Dec. 2000

Merry Christmas
to Cassie &
Love, Carol Jean Coombs

Under a Christmas Star

Under a Christmas Star

Stories for Christmas Eve

Compiled by

Carol Jean Cook Coombs

ISBN: 1-55517-476-0
v.2

Published by Bonneville Books

Distributed by:
925 North Main, Springville, UT 84663 • 801/489-4084

CFI Publishing and Distribution Since 1986
Cedar Fort, Incorporated
CFI Distribution • CFI Books • Council Press • Bonneville Books

Typeset by Virginia Reeder
Cover design by Adam Ford
Cover design © 2000 by Lyle Mortimer

Printed in the United States of America

Dedication

For Bob, my husband and fellow collector,
who encouraged me to save
inspiring stories
and helped me at every stage of this book.

My thanks to

Kate Coombs, my daughter,
for her creative suggestions and editing.

Loni, Karen, Holly and Krista, my other daughters,
and Bob and David, my sons,
for being enthusiastic listeners.

Gracia Stewart Cook, my mother,
for inspiring a love of reading.

David William Cook, my father,
for teaching me how to tell stories.

Sherron Robinson, my cousin,
for encouraging me to publish these stories.

Carla Cronkhite Vera, my co-worker at UCLA,
for evaluating and typing the manuscript.

Table of Contents

III. Morning of Miracles

IV. And On Earth Peace

Prologue

In our family, Christmas Eve was a time for songs and stories. We crowded around the piano to sing "Winter Wonderland" and "Joy to the World," "Silver Bells" and "Silent Night." Every year the Narrator read the timeless Christmas story from the pages of Matthew and Luke as whichever children were the right sizes acted the parts. (While our family was still small, our oldest son often played the donkey, the shepherds, and the wise men!)

There were other stories, too, reflecting the light of that first Christmas star. Each year I brought out a box of Christmas books to read during the season. Then on Christmas Eve, sitting in the firelight, I told our favorite Christmas stories to a rapt audience of children and eventually grandchildren. When I asked our grown daughters what their best childhood memories were, one replied, "The stories on Christmas Eve." They thought that you, too, would like them.

During World War II, a German boy and his brother were conscripted into the Army. They were soon separated—Alfred was sent to North Africa and his brother to Russia. Before they parted, they made a pact, a promise that at every day's end each would look up into the night sky for the North Star. When he saw it, he would say a prayer for his brother, remembering that he was not alone. He would find comfort in knowing that somewhere in the darkness, his brother lifted his eyes to the same star and his heart to the same God, who would watch over them both.

Christmas helps us remember that we are not alone, that God is a loving Father who watches over us. Stories of Christmas help us, like these young soldiers, lift our eyes to the heavens, lift our hearts in greater kindness and our thoughts in higher hope. We remember Christ, "the bright and morning star" (Revelation 22: 16).

I

A Child's Gift

The best Christmas stories, like the first one, are about children. Our family Christmas celebration caught its breath a little during the teenage years, buried under an avalanche of trendy clothes. Now the grandchildren play with the ribbons and wrapping paper, exclaim over the colored lights, and give us home-made treasures. Is there anything sweeter than a child's gift?

One of my most memorable gifts came from two little daughters, ages 9 and 11. Loni and Kate wanted to give me something truly wonderful, and noticed I needed a new watch. They rode their bikes to the local jeweler's and looked at the most affordable watches—$20 was quite a bit of money for two little girls in the mid-seventies. These watches were nice, but there were prettier watches up on the shelf. They set their sights higher. "How much are those?" Their favorite cost $54—a small fortune.

They carefully calculated whether they could somehow buy this marvel, all by themselves, without resorting to their father, who provided a small allowance for babysitting and other chores. It had been their custom to ride their bikes to the library every week, stopping along the way at Dave's Doo-Bee-Doo for a hot dog and soda lunch. They decided that if they skipped their treat every week for the months remaining before Christmas—saved all their money and earned more to boot—they could buy the beautiful watch. Instead of lunch, their new ritual was to visit the watch each Saturday at the jeweler's, where a kind clerk was saving it for them.

When two excited little girls gave me their gift and I unwrapped it to see a watch-shaped box, their father and I glanced at each other knowingly—they must have tucked something else inside. But I lifted the lid, and there it lay, the most beautiful watch I had ever seen. To this day it is one of my treasures.

As Jesus said of little children, "Of such are the kingdom of heaven." These five stories show the pure joy of Christmas glowing in the generous hearts of children.

Trouble at the Inn

by

Dina Donahue

For years now, whenever Christmas pageants are talked about in a certain little town in the Midwest, someone is sure to mention the name of Wallace Purling. Wally's performance in one annual production of the Nativity play has slipped into the realm of legend. But the old-timers who were in the audience that night never tire of recalling exactly what happened.

Wally was nine that year and in the second grade, though he should have been in the fourth. Most people in town knew that he had difficulty in keeping up. He was big and clumsy, slow in movement and mind. Still, Wally was well liked by the other children in his class, all of whom were smaller than he, though the boys had trouble hiding their irritation when the uncoordinated Wally would ask to play ball with them.

Most often they'd find a way to keep him off the field, but Wally would hang around anyway—not sulking, just hoping. He was always a helpful boy, a willing and smiling one, and the natural protector, paradoxically, of the underdog. Sometimes if the older boys chased the younger ones away, it would always be Wally who'd say, "Can't they stay? They're no bother."

Wally fancied the idea of being a shepherd with a

---

flute in the Christmas pageant that year, but the play's director, Miss Lumbard, assigned him to a more important role. After all, she reasoned, the innkeeper did not have too many lines, and Wally's size would make his refusal of lodging to Joseph more forceful.

And so it happened that the usual large, partisan audience gathered for the town's Yuletide extravaganza of the crooks and creches, of beards, crowns, halos, and a whole stage full of squeaking voices. No one on stage or off was more caught up in the magic of the night than Wallace Purling. They said later that he stood in the wings and watched the performance with such fascination that from time to time Miss Lumbard had to make sure he didn't wander on stage before his cue.

Then the time came when Joseph appeared, slowly, tenderly guiding Mary to the door of the inn. Joseph knocked hard on the wooden door set into the painted backdrop. Wally the innkeeper was there, waiting.

"What do you want?" Wally said, swinging the door open with a brusque gesture.

"We seek lodging."

"Seek it elsewhere." Wally looked straight ahead but spoke vigorously. "The inn is filled."

"Sir, we have asked everywhere in vain. We have traveled far and are very weary."

"There is no room in this inn for you." Wally looked properly stern.

"Please, good innkeeper, this is my wife, Mary. She is heavy with child and needs a place to rest. Surely you must have some small corner for her. She is so tired."

Now, for the first time, the innkeeper relaxed his stiff stance and looked down at Mary. With that, there was a long pause, long enough to make that audience a bit tense with embarrassment.

"No! Be gone!" the prompter whispered from the

wings.

"No!" Wally repeated automatically. "Be gone!"

Joseph sadly placed his arm around Mary and Mary laid her head upon her husband's shoulder and the two of them started to move away. The innkeeper did not return inside his inn, however. Wally stood there in the doorway, watching the forlorn couple. His mouth was open, his brow creased with concern, his eyes filling unmistakably with tears.

And suddenly this Christmas pageant became different from all others.

"Don't go, Joseph," Wally called out. "Bring Mary back." And Wallace Purling's face grew into a bright smile. "You can have my room...."

A Christmas Gift I'll Never Forget

by

L.D. Hummel

He entered my life 20 years ago, leaning against the doorjamb of Room 202, where I taught fifth grade. He wore sneakers three sizes too large and checkered pants ripped at the knees.

Daniel, as I'll call him, though that was not his real name, made this undistinguished entrance in the school of a quaint lakeside village known for its old money, white colonial homes and brass mailboxes. He told me his last school had been in a neighboring county. "We were pickin' fruit," he said matter-of-factly.

I suspected this friendly, scruffy, smiling boy from a migrant family had no idea he had been thrown into a den of fifth-grade lions who had never before seen torn pants. If he noticed snickering, he didn't let on. There was no chip on his shoulder.

Twenty-five children eyed Daniel suspiciously until the kickball game that afternoon. Then he led off the first inning with a home run. With it came a bit of respect from the wardrobe critics of Room 202.

Next was Charles' turn. Charles was the least athletic, most overweight child in the history of fifth grade. After his second strike, amid the rolled eyes and groans of the class, Daniel edged up and spoke quietly to

---

Charles' dejected back. "Forget them, kid. You can do it."

Charles warmed, smiled, stood taller and promptly struck out anyway. But at that precise moment, defying the social order of this jungle he had entered, Daniel had gently begun to change things—and us.

By autumn's end, we had all gravitated toward him. He taught us all kinds of lessons. How to call a wild turkey. How to tell whether fruit is ripe before that first bite. How to treat others, even Charles. Especially Charles. He never did use our names, calling me "Miss" and the students "kid."

The day before Christmas vacation, the students always brought gifts for the teacher. It was a ritual—opening each department store box, surveying the expensive perfume or scarf or leather wallet, and thanking the child.

That afternoon, Daniel walked to my desk and bent close to my ear. "Our packing boxes came out last night," he said without emotion. "We're leavin' tomorrow."

As I grasped the news, my eyes filled with tears. He countered the awkward silence by telling me about the move. Then, as I regained my composure, he pulled a gray rock from his pocket. Deliberately and with great style, he pushed it gently across my desk.

I sensed that this was something remarkable, but all my practice with perfume and silk had left me pitifully unprepared to respond. "It's for you," he said, fixing his eyes on mine. "I polished it up special."

I've never forgotten that moment.

Years have passed since then. Each Christmas my daughter asks me to tell this story. It always begins after she has picked up the small polished rock that sits on my desk and nestled herself in my lap. The first words of the story never vary. "The last time I ever saw Daniel, he gave me this rock as a gift and told me about his boxes. That was a long time ago, even before you were born.

"He's a grownup now," I finish. Together we wonder where he is and what he has become.

"Someone good I bet," my daughter says. Then she adds, "Do the end of the story."

I know what she wants to hear—the lesson of love and caring learned by a teacher from a boy with nothing—and everything—to give. A boy who lived out of boxes. I touch the rock, remembering.

"Hi kid," I say softly. "This is Miss: I hope you no longer need the packing boxes. And Merry Christmas, wherever you are."

Christmas Day in the Morning

by

Pearl Buck

He woke suddenly and completely. It was four o'clock, the hour at which his father had always called him to get up and help with the milking. Strange how the habits of his youth clung to him still! Fifty years ago, and his father had been dead for thirty years, and yet he awoke at four o'clock in the morning. He had trained himself to turn over and go to sleep, but this morning it was Christmas, he did not try to sleep.

Why did he feel so awake tonight? He slipped back in time, as he did so easily nowadays. He was fifteen years old and still on his father's farm. He loved his father. He had not known it until one day a few days before Christmas, when he had overheard what his father was saying to his mother.

"Mary, I hate to call Rob in the mornings. He's growing so fast and he needs his sleep. If you could see how he sleeps when I go in to wake him up! I wish I could manage alone."

"Well, you can't, Adam." His mother's voice was brisk, "Besides, he isn't a child anymore. It's time he took his turn."

"Yes," his father said slowly. "But I sure do hate to wake him."

When he heard these words, something in him woke: his father loved him! He had never thought of it before, taking for granted the tie of their blood. Neither his father nor his mother talked about loving their children—they had no time for such things. There was always so much to do on the farm.

Now that he knew his father loved him, there would be no more loitering in the mornings and having to be called again. He got up after that, stumbling blind with sleep, and pulled on his clothes, his eyes tight shut, but he got up.

And then on the night before Christmas, that year when he was fifteen, he lay for a few minutes thinking about the next day. They were poor, and most of the excitement was in the turkey they had raised themselves and the mince pies his mother made. His sisters sewed presents and his mother and father always bought something he needed, not only a warm jacket, maybe, but something more, such as a book. And he saved and bought them each something, too.

He wished, that Christmas he was fifteen, he had a better present for his father. As usual, he had gone to the ten-cent store and bought a tie. It had seemed nice enough until he lay thinking the night before Christmas. He looked out of his attic window, the stars were bright.

"Dad," he had once asked when he was a little boy, "What is a stable?"

"It's just a barn," his father had replied, "like ours."

Then Jesus had been born in a barn, and to a barn the shepherds had come...

The thought struck him like a silver dagger. Why should he not give his father a special gift too, out there in the barn? He could get up early, earlier than four o'clock, and he could creep into the barn and get all the milking done. He'd do it alone, milk and clean up, and then when his father went in to start the milking he'd see it all done. And he would know who had done it. He laughed to himself as he gazed at the stars. It was what he would do, and he mustn't sleep too soundly.

He must have awakened twenty times, scratching a match each time to look at his old watch—midnight, and half past one, and then two o'clock.

At a quarter to three he got up and put on his clothes. He crept downstairs, careful of the creaky boards, and let himself out. The cows looked at him, sleepy and surprised. It was early for them too.

He had never milked all alone before, but it seemed almost easy. He kept thinking about his father's surprise. His father would come in and get him, saying that he would get things started while Rob was getting dressed. He'd go to the barn, open the door, and then he'd go to get the two big empty milk cans. But they wouldn't be waiting or empty; they'd be standing in the milkhouse, filled.

"What the..." he could hear his father exclaiming.

He smiled and milked steadily, two strong streams rushing into the pail, frothing and fragrant.

The task went more easily than he had ever known it to go before. Milking for once was not a chore. It was something else, a gift to his father who loved him. He finished, the two milk cans were full, and he covered them and closed the milkhouse door carefully, making sure of the latch.

Back in his room he had only a minute to pull off his clothes in the darkness and jump into bed, for he heard his father up. He put the covers over his head to silence his quick breathing. The door opened.

"Rob!" His father called. "We have to get up, son, even if it is Christmas."

"Aw-right," he said sleepily.

The door closed and he lay still, laughing to himself.

In just a few minutes his father would know. His dancing heart was ready to jump from his body.

The minutes were endless—ten, fifteen, he did not know how many—and he heard his father's footsteps again. The door opened and he lay still.

"Rob!"

"Yes, Dad...."

His father was laughing, a queer sobbing sort of a laugh.

"Thought you'd fool me, did you?" His father was standing beside his bed, feeling for him, pulling away the cover.

"It's for Christmas, Dad!"

He found his father and clutched him in a great hug. He felt his father's arms go around him. It was dark and they could not see each other's face.

"Son, I thank you. Nobody ever did a nicer thing...."

"Oh, Dad, I want you to know—I do want to be good!" The words broke from him of their own will. He did not know what to say. His heart was bursting with love.

He got up and pulled on his clothes again and they went down to the Christmas tree. Oh, what a Christmas, and how his heart had nearly burst again with shyness and pride as his father told his mother and made the younger children listen about how he, Rob, had got up all by himself.

"The best Christmas gift I ever had, and I'll remember it, son, every year on Christmas morning, so long as I live."

They had both remembered it, and now that his father was dead, he remembered it alone: that blessed Christmas dawn when, alone with the cows in the barn, he had made his first gift of true love.

This Christmas he wanted to write a card to his wife

and tell her how much he loved her, it had been a long time since he had really told her, although he loved her in a very special way, much more than he ever had when they were young. He had been fortunate that she had loved him. Ah, that was the true joy of life, the ability to love! Love was still alive in him, it still was.

It occurred to him suddenly that it was alive because long ago it had been born in him when he knew his father loved him. That was it: love alone could awaken love. And he could give the gift again and again. This morning, this blessed Christmas morning, he would give it to his beloved wife. He could write it down in a letter for her to read and keep forever. He went to his desk and began his love letter to his wife: My dearest love....

Such a happy, happy, Christmas!

Rich in Christmas Spirit

by

Angela Gionfriddo

It was the last day before Christmas break at the school where I was a teacher's aide. One after the other, the first-graders filed in, presenting gaily wrapped presents to me and the teacher.

Last in line was a boy named Rashad who was clutching something close to his chest. I noticed his peculiar walk and realized he felt embarrassed as he quickly thrust a package at me.

Loosely wrapped in the school's brown paper towels was a tray with orange juice, milk, cereal and a piece of fruit. "I didn't have any money to buy you a gift so I used one of my food tickets to get you breakfast this morning," he said.

I was overwhelmed by his generosity. With one small, unselfish gesture, a little boy had reminded me that Christmas wasn't about spending money, but about giving from the heart.

"Rich in Christmas Spirit" by Angela Gionfriddo. First published in *Woman's Day*, December 21, 1991.

Carla's Gift

by

Torey Hayden

You almost didn't notice her in class. She was small for seven, and quiet; she didn't cause trouble the way the boys did. Her features were plain, and her blond hair was cropped short in a ragged, home-cut style vaguely reminiscent of the Little Prince. No matter what the time of year, she always wore the same assortment of faded cotton dresses, the same cheap sneakers. Her name was Carla.

My specialty was behavioral disorders, although my class this year wasn't a traditional class for emotionally disturbed youngsters. Most of my seven students—six boys and Carla—were simply victims of abject poverty.

All 73 youngsters in the old sandstone school building were in special education. The floor below me housed two preschool programs. Our floor had a class for mentally handicapped six to nine year olds taught by my colleague, Maia, and my own class.

Carla should have been in with Maia. The tests administered in kindergarten gave Carla an IQ of 69—our school district rated any score below 70 as indicative of a mental handicap. But I had fewer students than Maia did, and Carla had a speech problem. By virtue of my interest in psychologically-based language difficulties, I had become the school's unofficial speech expert.

Carla's talents were not many. She couldn't read. She was hopeless at art. She couldn't even stick the ends of paper strips together to make chains. And the simplest math activities defeated her.

"Here, see what I have here?" I said to her one morning, and laid out 12 wooden cubes. "Can you count these?"

"One, one, one..." she struggled.

I put a hand over hers and moved it along as I counted. "One, two, three..."

"Four, five, six..." she continued alone, "seven, nine, ten, eleven..."

"Whoops, Carla you've left out eight. One, two..."

"Three, four, five, six, seven, nine..."

"Whoops, you've left out eight again. Here. Do it with me." I covered her hand and moved it along the cubes.

"One, two, three, four, five, six, seven, eight, nine, ten, eleven, twelve. What comes after seven?"

"Eight," she said. "Eight, eight, eight."

"Good. Now you try it by yourself."

Carla hesitated and then began. "One, two, three, four, five, six, seven, eight, ten, eleven, twelve!"

"Whoops. Carla, you've left out nine..."

I tried to be understanding, but I didn't have Maia's patience working with such a slow student. With the boys' clamoring for attention—their minds lively, if not sharp—I sometimes resented the time Carla required to learn something. I knew however much time I put in, I wouldn't get much out of her. Carla just didn't have much to give.

Christmas was a big event in our school. Because so many children came from poor families, many homes would have no tree and few presents. And with so many broken families, no festive gatherings.

We attempted to catch the best of the holiday spirit at school. We tried to emphasize simple pleasures—that there is more to Christmas (even to the secularized version we celebrated in school) than the gaudy commercialism presented on television. This inspired a good deal of creativity as we too were on a very limited budget.

One of the service clubs in town provided us with a large Christmas tree, which we erected in the gym and decorated with sugar cookies. Another provided a Santa Claus and a sackful of toys for our party on the last day before the Christmas vacation. The members collected secondhand toys every year and renovated them, so the gifts given out during the party were nice and, for many of the children, would likely be the only toys they received. As a consequence, we on the staff did our best to match the toys with appropriate children. The best way we found was to have the kids write letters to Santa.

My group, of course, was enthusiastic when letter-writing time came around. Mikey, a rather streetwise six-year-old, snatched up his paper. "I know what I'm going to ask for. One of them four-wheel dirt bikes."

"That's too big for Santa to bring, don't you think, Mikey?" I asked. "He only has one sack to hold all the gifts. I doubt a dirt bike would fit."

"Santa Claus is just a big fake-o anyway," Nathan announced. Nathan was eight, and worldly.

I sat down beside Carla, who was having trouble copying "Dear Santa" from the blackboard. "What do you hope Santa brings you?" I asked.

"Red," she said. "Red, red, red. Balloon. Birthday balloon."

"A balloon?"

"Red balloon. Go up, up, up."

"A balloon?" Nathan shouted. "You want just a balloon for Christmas? What a stupid idea!"

"Nathan! Shush!" I said to him.

"Birthday balloon," Carla said. "Christmas Jesus birthday."

"Yes, it is. That's why we celebrate Christmas, isn't it? But what would you like Santa to bring? A doll, perhaps? A game?"

"Red, red, red," she said impatiently. "Birthday balloon."

My aide, Rosa, who was working nearby with one of the boys, lifted her head and smiled sadly at me. Carla would be one of those children for whom there would probably be no celebration beyond what we offered at school. She had no father. Her mother's boyfriend had just gone up for seven years in the penitentiary on drug charges. I realized that to Carla even a red balloon might seem an extravagance.

After school Rosa and I discussed the matter, "I'll tuck a balloon in," I said. "I think I have some left over from Nathan's birthday."

"I want her to get a nice present," Rosa said. "Maybe a little doll. Something to play with."

On the afternoon of the party, the children were in a frenzy of excitement. At 1:30, Santa arrived, ho-ho-ho-ing his way into the gym and dragging an enormous bag full of presents. The children screamed with pleasure and surrounded him.

"This is really going to be good," Rosa whispered. "I love this. I love seeing their expressions." Sharing her enjoyment, I settled into a chair to watch. First one, then another of the children received their gifts, oohing as they opened them and running over to us to show them off.

"Here comes Carla's," Rosa said, as Santa Claus lifted out a big parcel and put it into Carla's waiting hands. For several moments Carla did nothing but hold it out at arm's length and regard the gift wrapping.

"Look at her," Rosa said with affection. "She's overwhelmed."

Indeed, she appeared to be, so I got up and went over. "What have you got there?" I asked and knelt beside her. "Do you want to open it?"

Hunkering down on the floor, Carla ripped off the wrapping. Inside was a big brown teddy bear. "Oh, what a wonderful present!" I said.

Carla began to cry. "No balloon. No birthday balloon."

"There's a balloon here, sweetheart. Look...." I rummaged through the paper to pull out the red balloon we'd included with the bear.

"No." Carla wept. "Birthday balloon go up, up, up."

"I can blow it up...." I began, and then it dawned on me. "A helium balloon? You wanted one that floats?"

She nodded through her tears.

There were 35 minutes left to the school day. I turned to Rosa. "Can you keep track of things? I'm going to try and get Carla a helium balloon."

"From where?"

"I don't know. But I'll be back before the end." Grabbing the red balloon, I headed out to my car.

I tried the dime store, the drugstore, the card shop and finally a gas station. Yes, the attendant said, they had helium: $53 for a small bottle with a $20 deposit to insure that I brought the bottle back. I only want to blow up one balloon, I explained. Sorry, he said. Come on, I pleaded—it's Christmas. At last he relented and filled the balloon for me. I roared back to school with it, just in time.

Carla's face, when she saw the red balloon, made all my efforts worthwhile. She ran pell-mell across the gymnasium to fling her arms around my waist. I grabbed a discarded piece of ribbon and tied it to the balloon, then handed it to her. "Here you are. Santa forgot to bring this in for you."

Smiling gloriously, she let the balloon float gently upward. "Birthday balloon," she crooned. "Up, up, up."

Then it was time to put on boots and coats, to collect goodies and go home. As I helped the boys get ready, Carla sat on the bench in the cloakroom and played with the balloon, letting it rise, pulling it down, letting it rise again.

"Carla, time to go."

"Carla's dorky," Mikey said. "It's just a balloon."

"It's 'cause she's nothing but a retard," Nathan replied.

I gripped Nathan's collar and spun him around the corner into the classroom to have a few words with him, but Carla still sat, oblivious, and played with her balloon.

After seeing the boys down to their rides, I returned to the cloakroom. "Carla, come on. Your bus is here." I helped her on with her coat. "Here, get your scarf on, too. It's cold out." She watched the balloon bounce as she tugged the ribbon. "Let's go. I'll walk you down."

"Birthday balloon," she was murmuring to herself. "Happy birthday."

Her bus was parked at the far end of the drive, but she didn't hurry. She was holding the balloon in front of her and gazing up. Then, without warning, she let go. The breeze caught it and sailed it upward.

"Carla!" I cried in dismay. "Now look what's happened!" All that trouble I'd gone to, and she'd simply let the balloon go. I felt like yelling at her. Christmas or no.

But Carla only stood, watching the balloon rise high in the gray December sky. "Up, up, up," she whispered. "Birthday balloon up in sky."

"Yes, it's up in the sky, all right," I muttered gloomily.

"Happy birthday, baby Jesus," she said. "Happy birthday." And she turned to me and smiled.

II

I Was A Stranger

My mother, who collects gem-like quotations and shares them with her children, recently sent me this one: "The most important thing in life is to learn to give out love and to let it come in." At Christmas, most of us think of giving love to family and friends. But sometimes love is best learned unexpectedly, when strangers reach out to each other.

My husband and I used to live in an apartment near the university where we work. Walking back and forth through the nearby commercial village, we often passed a woman sitting in a lawn chair hoping for handouts. She insisted on giving a Tootsie pop to anyone who gave her some change. "Don't throw it away," she would say. "Eat it. It's really good." Then one day, as I came up the street, I saw this woman from some distance away stand awkwardly on her red, swollen legs. She made her way over to a bus bench where a homeless man lay. As I drew closer, I saw her speak to him and give him something. Sitting back down, she saw me watching her. "I gave him some money," she explained a little self-consciously. "It's really awful not to have any money."

One anonymous carol-writer has called the infant Christ "the wondrous little Stranger" ("With Wondering Awe"). The stories in this section remind us of what Christ said about people who reach out to help those in need:

> *I was an hungered, and ye gave me meat; I was thirsty, and ye gave me drink; I was a stranger, and ye took me in...*(Matthew 25: 35).

May we remember to take Him in—finding room for Him and for "the least of these our brethren."

How Santa Spread Cheer Without Eight Tiny Reindeer

by

Rip Rense

It was not a season to be very jolly. My father and stepmother had been arguing for several days about whether I was to visit my mother for Christmas. My stepmother opposed it; my father felt it was necessary. The tension eventually became so thick that I lost whatever interest I had in making the trip. I was ten and figured, of course, I was the cause of the problem.

I hadn't seen my mother for a couple years and felt awkward about visiting her. But my dad prevailed and, like it or not, I would spend Christmas Eve with Mom and then return home December 25 for the "real" Christmas. I was deposited at the Greyhound bus station in Thousand Oaks with a paper sack containing two changes of clothes. Next stop: Newport Beach.

The trip took about six hours, which didn't bother me much because, for the first time in my life, I was out of reach of all parents. I had fantasies of the bus heading straight to South America. They'd never see me again!

When we finally reached Newport, I disembarked and followed the other travelers into the station, inhaling that eau de old cigarette butts, Lysol and lingering diesel exhaust peculiar to bus station lobbies. I found a pay

---

phone and told a gravel-voiced taxi dispatcher that I had to get to the Newporter Inn Hotel, where my mom worked nights as a cashier. The gravel voice told me to sit tight and my ride would be there soon.

As I waited, I watched my fellow passengers being met by smiling friends and relatives who whisked them off, no doubt, to purring cats, crackling fireplaces and shiny packages under twinkling trees.

Finally, the only other person left in the station was a ticket agent nodding off over a book. I looked outside. No cab. I was stranded, apparently, forgotten and abandoned.

I considered hoofing it, but just as I was about to venture down the highway, a beat-up yellow Plymouth chugged into a far corner of the parking lot and stopped in the near darkness. Was that wreck my cab? It had to be. I grabbed my bag and hurried through the lot, pulling out my wallet to get the fare.

And discovered that no one had given me so much as a dollar.

This called for sheer panic. I had to get to my mom's place. Maybe I could just bolt from the cab when we reached the hotel and run like hell.

No, they'd catch me and throw me in jail and then neither my mom nor dad would ever find me again—at least until after Christmas. I had to tell the truth. As I approached the Plymouth, ready to plead my case, the rear passenger door swung opened and a husky voice shot from the shadowy interior:

"You call a taxi?"

"Uh, yea."

I was too intimidated by the voice to mention my empty wallet.

"Well, get in."

I scrambled into the back seat with my paper bag

suitcase. Trapped with a stranger in a dark car, far from home, broke, destined for kidnapping, or at least prosecution for non-payment of fare. But the door was closed. We were rolling, so I could only settle in, when what to my wondering eyes should appear but, well....

Santa Claus was driving the taxi.

"Ho Ho! So, where ya going?"

His great white whiskers moved up and down as he spoke, and his ruddy cheeks glowed in the rear-view mirror. The bell on the end of his scarlet cap tinkled, and his black leather-gloved hands squeaked as they gripped the steering wheel. It was St. Nick, all right.

"Where you headed, m' boy?"

"Uhh...Newporter Inn.... Do you know...?"

"Ho Ho! Of course I know where it is."

And away we went, me and Santa Claus in a smoking old Plymouth barreling down the Pacific Coast Highway in Newport Beach, California, one crisp December evening back in 1963.

"So if you don't mind my asking," he said, "what are you doing on a bus at Christmas time?"

I shyly explained the vagaries of my home life. He reacted kindly, as though there was nothing unusual about it. This put me more at ease, and I noticed for the first time a book resting on his dashboard. "Milton Cross's Stories of Great Operas." I happened to know who Milton Cross was because my dad listened to Cross host the Metropolitan Opera broadcast every Saturday during the Met's season, at such volume that no one in the house could avoid it.

"Is that a good book?" I said. "I like opera."

"You do? A lad like you? What's your favorite?"

I probably said "La Boheme" or "Die Walkure." They were the only ones I knew by title.

"Really? So you like singing...Say, have you ever

heard a Russian Christmas carol?"

"Uhh...No."

"How would you like to hear one?"

"Sure."

With that, Santa rolled down the window, tilted his head back, and broke into a rich, opulent bass that filled every square inch of space inside the cab. The words were hearty and full of earthy Russian diphthongs; the robust melody was poignant. As we sailed through the salty ocean air and glistening lights, past gas stations and Christmas tree lots, Santa's basso profundo and bouncing beard caused heads in passing cars to turn and stare.

"I sing a little opera with a local company," he explained after finishing the song. "I'm a bass-baritone. Want to hear another one?"

I was so amazed I could barely speak.

"Sure."

He sang all the way to the circular driveway of the Newporter Inn, where I finally, guiltily, got the nerve to confess that somebody had forgotten to give me money for cab fare, but that if he'd only trust me for a minute, I'd run inside just as fast as I could and get some money from my mom. Really.

I saw his eyes smiling in the rearview mirror.

"Don't you know?" he said. "When Santa drives, nobody pays."

I sat, not quite understanding.

"On Christmas Eve, there's only one of us in all the taxis," he said turning around, hanging a red-sleeved elbow over the back of the seat, "and if you get the cab with Santa Claus, you ride for free."

While I sat there trying to figure out if this was company policy or something ethereal, he held out his hand.

"So Merry Christmas to you!" he said.

"Oh, thanks," I answered haltingly, shaking the black leather glove. "Thanks. And um...Merry Christmas to you." I stepped out.

And as the cab disappeared into the night, I caught a glimpse of the fluffy white beard moving up and down again, and could hear through the open window, the strains of another mellifluent Russian Christmas carol. Which must have translated, more or less, to:

"Merry Christmas to all, and to all a good night."

Then We Found the Rocking Horse

by

Derek Dixon

The house was very quiet. My wife and three teenage daughters had gone to the first of the end-of-year sales in search of clothing bargains. I sat alone in a deep armchair, an unread book on my knees, looking at the snow-covered lawn where we had found the rocking horse fifteen days before. I was remembering those ten hectic days before Christmas when a simple family council resolution had opened so many hearts in what had seemed an iron-hearted town.

Wendy had said from the pinnacle of her twelve years, "Christmas isn't like it used to be, is it? There used to be a funny feeling around the house, all warm and cozy and safe, but I can't feel it any more." The others chimed in with their remarks and a pattern began to emerge. Our recent Christmases had failed because of too much eating, too much television watching, too much wrangling over petty things, too many late nights and late rising, and too much concern for self.

And it looked as though the coming Christmas was going to be the same—a spiritual and family failure. The days would pass and again we would have that terrible, dried out, flat feeling. Was there no way to change the nature of the season in our home? No way to recapture the true spirit of Christmas?

A pause came in the council, and then my wife began to tell us about some young patients at the school for mentally handicapped children where she worked as a physiotherapist several hours a week. She spoke of emotional deprivation, of uncaring parents, of pinching poverty in many homes, of being forgotten because "they only smash things, don't they?" and of little hands empty at the time of giving.

My wife proposed that we, as a family, gather toys for those forgotten children at the school. Approval of her suggestion was unanimous.

The following day we put our plan into effect. We explained to our friends about the children at the school and asked them for any little gifts they might care to contribute.

We received one or two stony stares and some half-promises—beyond that, nothing. We had only recently moved to that neighborhood, and had scoffed at remarks that the town was a hard town, full of seemingly materialistic, hard-hearted people. Now it seemed to be more than true.

Disappointed at the lack of contributions, we decided that at least we would make a contribution of our own; and so for the next few evenings, after supper was over, we set to making little dolls' beds out of plywood and hardboard, which we then painted in bright gloss paint; my wife supplied miniature mattresses and covers. The kitchen began to look like a Lilliputian army supply base! We made six beds in all.

Still nothing from others, still we asked. Only six days left to Christmas.

On the fifth day we found a rocking horse standing on the back lawn, shimmering in sunshine and frost, his mane worn but triumphant, his eyes wild with the sight of battle, and in his ears the thunder of the captains and the shouting. On the ground beside him stood a cardboard soapbox full of assorted toys. To this day their coming is a mystery to us. And yet it seemed to be a sign, for that very day people began arriving at the front door with gifts for the forgotten children at the school.

One distant neighbor, a single man, lonely and stiff, a man not even invited to contribute, crossed the street to my wife and blurted out:

"Look here, I haven't anything moneywise; but I have been saving little toy motor cars in matchboxes. I get them from the garage. Every time I buy six gallons of petrol, they present me with another motor car. I've got 20 altogether. Well, no man has ever asked me to help in something like this, so I'd like to do my bit now. I'll bring the motor cars along to your house tomorrow night and you can be Santa Claus for me."

And he turned away to hide his embarrassment; but when the following evening came, he was there on the step with his 20 motor cars.

An even greater surprise waited at my office. One young man had been reared in London's harsh East End—a man of prejudice and heated temper to whom my attempts to live my religion were a waving flag to a bull. But that day he came to me and said:

"You and I are no great friends—in fact, I wouldn't help you to the end of the street if you had both big toes fractured; but those children at the school are something different. I see their faces every time I close my eyes. Ginny and I were talking about them and wondering how we could help; and we've decided to give the best we have. In my spare moments, I model and paint airplanes. We hang them from the ceiling at home and admire then from time to time; but beyond that they do nothing, so we thought we would give those. And what does it matter if the kids do smash them up playing with them? An hour's pleasure for such a child is well worth the loss of a few models to us."

That very afternoon he produced a large selection of model airplanes.

When I arrived home that evening, my wife and children had similar experiences to relate—of shy strangers and generous enemies—and of friends, too—all of whom were haunted by visions of the empty-handed children; our front room overflowed with their gifts.

The following day the school van called at our home, and the gifts were loaded on board and delivered to the headmistress to distribute to the children. And that was that.

None of those who contributed gifts ever asked for or received recognition or thanks. At the school, only the headmistress ever knew from where the gifts had come. The rest was silence.

But as I sit here in the twilight after Christmas, I wonder if the spirit that permeates our home permeates theirs. For we, as a family, found again in service to others the real spirit of Christmas. The very walls are alive with sweetness and calm.

And as the winter day moves toward its early close, and the cold stars stare down and the snow upon the lawn reflects back the light from my windows, I think upon the true nature of the universe: for from this small miracle at Christmas, I have learned that every act of man reaches out into the universe. Wheels turn, the gears mesh, eternal balances are set in motion, and the earth is changed by the little secrets of kindness that have no significance at all to any earthly historian.

Used Car Dealer Plays Santa

from

Ventura County Star Free Press

When Craig Bartlett and his two children set out in search of a $100 car, they didn't expect Santa Claus to show up in the form of a car dealer.

Bartlett's 1967 Chevrolet, badly damaged a month ago in an accident, stalled on the highway more than a mile from the Chevrolet dealer in White Bear Lake, Minn., who had advertised a $100 car.

So Bartlett wrapped up his children, Matthew, two, and Michele, five, in blankets and started walking. They finally made it to what Bartlett thought was Polar Chevrolet but which turned out to be White Bear Lincoln Mercury.

"I asked them if they had a $100 car and they said they didn't," Bartlett said, but they suggested he look around. "They showed me a Pinto and I said, `I'll take it for $100.'"

Salesman Bill McKnight went to get the title papers from Randy Lee, the dealership owner. When he returned he asked Bartlett if he would settle for $6.50.

"I thought it was $100?" Bartlett replied. McKnight told him, "Believe it or not, the owner said to sell it for $1. The $5.50 is for transferring the title."

McKnight said Bartlett's white, nearly rust-free 1973

Pinto was the first car he had seen given away in his 15 years in the business.

He said he and Lee took a look at Bartlett's kids wrapped in blankets walking down the highway and Lee, 35, who bought the dealership a year ago, said, "Give him a car."

"We sold it for $1 to make it legal," McKnight said, and told Bartlett to save the rest of the money for the kids for Christmas.

Bartlett is still incredulous about his luck. "Even the snow treads are new," he said. "They winterized it, the radio works, everything works! They even towed my beater to their lot."

The Two Festivals of Light

by

Leo Buscaglia

Christmas never fails to evoke memories. Most of us can recall Christmases of great joy and of disappointment, of warm camaraderie and of frightening loneliness, of exciting hellos and of painful good-byes.

It's strange how memory works—why we remember what we remember and forget what we forget. How is it that I can remember so vividly the details of a special Christmas more than fifty years ago, and forget important events of just a few days past?

I could not have been more than eight or nine years old on the Christmas when our new neighbors moved in. It was an exceptionally cold and rainy Los Angeles December. I remember it well because of the embarrassment I felt over having to wear my sister's winter coat, which she had outgrown. In our home, clothes were not thrown out, they were handed down, and it was my turn—no matter the girlish fur piping on the collar and sleeves and buttons on the wrong side.

We lived in a small house heated by a single wood-burning stove that served to separate the kitchen and the dining room. I remember how we huddled that December to dress by its heat. The house was framed, similar to many others that are still to be found in the Boyle Heights

---

area of Los Angeles. They were proudly referred to at the time as craftsman houses.

The families who lived on our street were mostly first-generation immigrants: Jews from Eastern Europe, Italians from southern Italy, Germans, and Mexicans. Few of them spoke much English, most had large families, all of them were poor.

Our new neighbors moved in early in December—a Rabbi and his family: a boy, Elijah, who was my age, and a girl, Sarah, a few years older. When I saw them for the first time, I pretended to be playing, but watched as their large old pieces of furniture were unloaded from the moving van and disappeared into the darkness behind their front door. I wondered what they'd be like, if they'd speak English, if they'd be friendly. As is usually the case under such circumstances, it was Elijah and I who were the first to talk. It always seems easier for children, for some reason. We were soon walking to school each day, fast becoming close friends. He was one of the few children who didn't laugh at my coat.

We were standing in the school yard waiting for the bell to ring one morning when the subject of the approaching holiday came up.

"What are you going to get for Christmas?" I asked Elijah.

"I don't believe in Christmas," he said simply.

I was stunned.

"Everybody believes in Christmas," I insisted.

"I'm Jewish. We don't," he answered matter-of-factly.

"Well, what do you believe in if you don't believe in Christmas?" I persisted.

"Lots of things. But not Christmas," he responded.

When something of any importance happened during the day in our lives, it was always shared with the family at our dinner table that evening. It was here that anxieties were lessened, mysteries solved, solutions arrived at. I couldn't wait to tell the startling news. Our new neighbors didn't believe in Christmas!

Mama and Papa were as mystified as I was at the news. They were not moved by my elder brother's explanation that Christmas is a religious holiday, that there are all kinds of beliefs in the world, that the Cohens had as much right not to believe in Christmas as we did to believe in it. After all, he reasoned further, wasn't that part of why so many people left their homelands to emigrate to the United States?

Mama in her innocent wisdom rationalized, "Maybe they don't know about it. They come from far away, like we do, and maybe no one told them yet."

"Well, they don't come from the moon," my brother laughed.

"Don't be so smart," my mother said, "or I'll send you to the moon!" Mama had a way of making a point. She turned to Papa across the table. "They should be invited to share Christmas with us," she said.

That was Mama's way of handling any problem—feed it! And there was always a place at the table for anyone at any time. Perhaps that's why so many of my fondest memories are associated with eating.

Within a week of their moving in, I was hired by Rabbi Cohen as the Sabbath boy: the Gentile who serves the family on their Sabbath. I was paid generously—a nickel a week for the job, a fortune for a poor kid at the time. It was very easy. I just had to turn on the lights when the family returned from the synagogue, move a few pots of food to the stove, and turn on the gas.

This, of course, became another mysterious subject for our table talk. "How come you have to do that? That's really strange."

A few weeks prior to Christmas I was serving the Cohens' Sabbath table. When I finished my ritual, I did as I had been instructed by Papa and invited Rabbi Cohen and his family to Christmas dinner at our home. Elijah had warned me that they wouldn't come.

Rabbi Cohen was a man not easily forgotten. He was of medium stature but appeared much larger than life, with his bespectacled alert dark eyes, his shocking mass of black hair, his dark beard, and his black clothing—all serving to accentuate the whiteness of his delicate face and hands. We all thought that he was the very image of the man on the Smith Brothers cough drop box.

In his deep, melodious voice he answered my invitation. "Ah," he said. "Ve vould like to come to your house and meet your mama and papa, but better I talk first to your papa."

"They don't talk English too good," I warned him. "That's why they asked me to invite you. They talk Italian."

"Vell," the rabbi said with a smile, "I don't talk too good, either. But ve'll understand each other. Vy not? Ve're neighbors."

When he was at home, Papa could always be found in his garden. Behind the house grew endless vegetables: onions, peppers, garlic, zucchini, carrots, lettuce, and whatever the seasonal vegetables or fruits were. The front of the house was always a profusion of flowers. It was especially lovely this Christmas season, with large bushes of poinsettias—double red, in full bloom.

Rabbi Cohen stopped Papa in his weeding a few days later. Elijah and I, now good friends, stood close by to watch the historic encounter.

"I'm Rabbi Cohen, your new neighbor."

"I know you jus-a move in," Papa said. 'Is-a good you jus-a move in."

"It's time ve should meet," Rabbi Cohen said, with his unique inflection. He shook Papa's hand warmly. "I vant to thank you for the invitation to be vis you and your family for Christmas dinner."

"It's-a all right," Papa said. "You and your family come. We gotta plenty to eat."

"That's a problem," the rabbi smiled. "You see, ve can only eat certain style foods. Ve run a kosher household."

"Well," said Papa, in the usual way he had of refusing to allow anything to present a problem. "We'll cook what-a you eat—kosher." Of course, Papa had no idea what kosher was. He was counting on Mama's usual creativity in the kitchen.

"Vell," replied Rabbi Cohen, "it's a little bit more complicated dan dat."

He proceeded to explain what a kosher household entails. Papa nodded understanding, but it became plain that evening at the dinner table, that he had understood very little of what the rabbi told him. What he concluded was that Jews ate differently from other people, that they did know what Christmas was all about, and that they too had a very special holiday in December called Hanukkah. But in spite of communication problems, Papa was delighted to tell us that the Cohens would be our guests for Christmas dinner and, in turn, we were invited to share their Hanukkah ceremony several nights later.

My elder sister was sent out to the nearby kosher market on Wabash and Evergreen with instructions to buy enough kosher food to satisfy at least ten people. Papa wanted to be sure there would be enough. Though we had very little money to spare, feeding our new neighbors was a very high priority.

My mother was delighted and intrigued when my sister returned with large bags of assorted foods in tightly sealed jars and containers marked "kosher." The grocer had helped her select a very special feast, indeed.

Both holiday visits were great successes. After surmounting various problems and supplying appropriate utensils of their own, the Cohens were very touched by the special dinner set before them. The Buscaglias devoured their Christmas feast with their accustomed gusto. There were gifts for the Cohens under the Christmas tree, and in the soft glow of Christmas lights we serenaded them with carols, in both English and Italian.

Each year Mama proudly displayed a traditional manger scene which was made up of several small hand-carved figures: Mary, Joseph, the infant Jesus, and a few shepherds, angels, and animals which she had managed to carry with her among the few possessions she brought from Italy. Over the manger was a tiny banner on which were printed the words "Pace sulla terra agli uomini di buon volonta."

During the evening Mrs. Cohen fingered each of the images tenderly, then asked, "What does the banner say, Mrs. Buscaglia?"

"Peace. Peace," Mama answered.

"Yes," Rabbi Cohen sighed. "Peace."

I can remember much laughter that night, but I recall more vividly the tears brought on by shared memories of "the old country." How much they missed the families left behind, the dear friends, the special foods now unavailable, the places of their childhood that perhaps they would never see again.

Several evenings later we sat in the Cohen's living room eating potato latkes, sharing small glasses of wine, and breaking bread—the challah. We watched in silence as Mrs. Cohen lit the last of the Hanukkah candles from the flame of the shammash—eight in all—until the menorah was ablaze with light. Mrs. Cohen looked beautiful in the bright candlelight. "Like a Madonna," my mother told her. "Oy vey," Mrs. Cohen said, "a Jewish Madonna!" We listened to the prayers and the songs. Rabbi Cohen had a beautiful basso voice that towered over the others in a strange harmony. We were all presented with Hanukkah gifts. We learned to spin the dreidel, a great game that produced much laughter.

When the time came for us to depart, Rabbi Cohen put his arm around my father's shoulder. "Hanukkah isn't Christmas, but like your Christmas, it's a time of a miracle, a Festival of Light," he explained. He told us it celebrates a rededication of their temple, a reminder to put away thoughts of revenge and battle and share love in peace with family and friends. "Just like it says on your manger—time for `Peace on earth to men of goodwill.'"

I can still visualize the moment when we departed from the Hanukkah celebration. Papa huddled us all together under umbrellas at the bottom of the Cohens' front porch. He turned and said, "Happy Hanukkah, cari amici." Rabbi Cohen, his family surrounding him, smiled down at us, "Merry Christmas, neighbors. Mazel tov!"

This was the beginning of a loving friendship between our two families that was to last more than thirty years. Thirty years in which so many things happened, none of which we could foretell during that first special season. Rabbi Cohen died one day on his way to shul. His heart simply stopped. My brothers and sisters, one by one, left home. Elijah got married and I was his best man. His sister went off to college to become a doctor. Mrs. Cohen went to live with her brother in New York. My parents sold the family home and moved into a small apartment nearer to my elder sister.

Beautiful memories recalled have a way of re-creating the original glow and warmth surrounding them. I feel them still, writing these thoughts, even after fifty years. I can settle back and yield to the feeling of love we radiated during that holiday, a love that will never die as long as there is one of us to remember.

"Happy Hanukkah, cari amici."

"Merry Christmas, neighbor. Mazel tov!"

III

Morning of Miracles

Miracles happen at Christmas. People seem different then, as if the star's magic light softens their eyes and strengthens their hearts. One Christmas season, a score of years ago, we were given the opportunity to bring two sisters ages nine and twelve from Korea into our family. "We don't have the money it will cost," I said to the social worker. "You will," he replied. And when it came time to pay, we did.

When we picked the girls up at the airport, they were tired and scared and hungry. The food we had carefully prepared to eat on the long drive home was unfamiliar to them. Tuna sandwiches were strange. Carrot cake was strange, but it was good and so were the chips. Since we didn't know a word of Korean, and they knew no English, we and our other children sang all the songs we knew, including children's songs learned at church. Our new daughters listened and ate and slept.

The next day, we tucked our Korean daughters into the car for a shopping trip to the mall. After a whispered consultation they began singing to us. The words were unfamiliar, but the melodies we recognized as the children's songs we had sung the day before. To our delight, we realized that we had the same religious heritage.

Faith itself can seem like a miracle, especially in the dark times, before the light flares bright. Hearts of faith forging on in the face of trouble—these are the ones for whom miracles blossom surprisingly, like roses in the snow. Here are the stories of four such hearts.

The Gold and Ivory Tablecloth

by

Rev. Howard C. Schade

At Christmas time, men and women everywhere gather in their churches to wonder anew at the greatest miracle the world has ever known. But the story I like to recall was not a miracle—exactly.

It happened to a pastor who was very young. His church was very old. Once, long ago, it had flourished. Famous men had preached from its pulpit, prayed before its altar. Rich and poor alike worshipped there and built it beautifully. Now the good days had passed from the section of town where it stood. But the pastor and his young wife believed in their run-down church. They felt that with paint, hammer, and faith they could get it in shape. Together they went to work.

But in late December a severe storm whipped through the river valley, and the worst blow fell on the little church—a huge chunk of rain-soaked plaster fell off the inside wall just behind the altar. Sorrowfully, the pastor and his wife swept away the mess, but they couldn't hide the ragged hole.

The pastor looked at it and had to remind himself quickly, "Thy will be done!" But his wife wept, "Christmas is only two days away!"

That afternoon the despirited couple attended the auction held for the benefit of a youth group. The auction-

---

eer opened a box and shook out of its folds a handsome gold-and-ivory lace tablecloth. It was a magnificent item, nearly fifteen feet long. But it, too, dated from a long-vanished era. Who, today, had any use for such a thing? There were a few half-hearted bids. Then the pastor was seized with what he thought was a great idea. He bid it in for six dollars and fifty cents.

He carried the cloth back to the church and tacked it up on the wall behind the altar. It completely hid the hole! And the extraordinary beauty of its shimmering handwork cast a fine, holiday glow over the chancel. It was a great triumph. Happily he went back to preparing his Christmas sermon.

Just before noon on the day of Christmas Eve, as the pastor was opening the church, he noticed a woman standing in the cold at the bus stop.

"The bus won't be here for forty minutes!" he called, and invited her into the church to get warm.

She told him that she had come from the city that morning to be interviewed for a job as governess to the children of one of the wealthy families in town but she had been turned down. A war refugee, her English was imperfect.

The woman sat down in a pew and chafed her hands and rested. After a while she dropped her head and prayed. She looked up as the pastor began to adjust the great ivory-and-gold lace cloth across the hole. She rose suddenly and walked up the steps of the chancel. She looked at the tablecloth. The pastor smiled and started to tell her about the storm damage, but she didn't seem to listen. She took up a fold of cloth and rubbed it between her fingers.

"It is mine!" she said. "It is my banquet cloth!" She lifted the corner and showed the surprised pastor that there were initials monogrammed on it. "My husband had the cloth made especially for me in Brussels! There could not be another like it."

For the next few minutes the woman and the pastor talked excitedly together. She explained that she was Viennese; that she and her husband had opposed the Nazis and had decided to leave the country. They were advised to go separately. Her husband put her on a train for Switzerland. They planned that he would join her as soon as he could arrange to ship their household goods across the border.

She never saw him again. Later she heard that he had died in a concentration camp.

"I have always felt that it was my fault—to leave without him," she said. "Perhaps these years of wandering have been my punishment!"

The pastor tried to comfort her and urged her to take the cloth with her. She refused. Then she went away.

As the church began to fill on Christmas Eve, it was clear that the cloth was going to be a great success. It had been skillfully designed to look its best by candlelight.

After the service, the pastor stood in the doorway; many people told him that the church looked beautiful. One gentle-faced, middle-aged man—he was the local clock and watch repairman—looked rather puzzled.

"It is strange," he said in his soft accent. "Many years ago my wife—God rest her—and I owned such a cloth. In our home in Vienna, my wife put it on the table"—and here he smiled— "only when the bishop came to dinner!"

The pastor suddenly became very excited. He told the jeweler about the woman who had been in the church earlier in the day.

The startled jeweler clutched the pastor's arm. "Can it be? Does she live?"

Together the two got in touch with the family who had interviewed her. Then, in the pastor's car they started for the city. And as Christmas Day was born, this man and his wife—who had been separated through so many saddened Yuletides—were reunited.

To all who heard this story, the joyful purpose of the storm that knocked a hole in the wall of the church was now quite clear. Of course, people said it was a miracle, and I think you will agree it was the season for it!

A Christmas Full of Determination

by

Emil Busch

Christmas...1938. It was a very cold, hard winter. We were living in a coal mining town in Pennsylvania. I was working for the WPA and earning a salary of $52 monthly. We were paid on the 7th and 25th of each month, $26 each payday. Our house payment was due, so that left me with $6 to buy food for three weeks and Christmas.

We had buried one little girl in September and my wife Nellie, choked up with tears, said, "Now we can't get our two little children even a doll or get a wreath for the baby's grave."

The only way I could increase my $6 was to invest it and this is what I did. I hitched a ride to Pittsburgh about 20 miles away. I went to a wholesale house and bought three dozen neckties. That took one day of my time. I had only three days to get back my investment. I had no money left, only faith in myself.

The first day out knocking on doors, I sold one necktie. The second day, none. My wife, Nellie began to cry and said: "Now we don't even have money for food. Can't even buy a wreath for the baby's grave or the kids a doll." I thought this situation over all night and as I left the next day I told Nellie, "Don't you worry. We will have a Christmas if I have to steal you one!"

Thinking it over, I realized there was only one place where there really was any money—in the stores. I began making rounds to them. I sold a few to get money for food, then began to trade. To the florist shop, I traded a tie for a wreath for the baby's grave. To the toy shop, for the dolls. To the fruit stand, for some fruit. To the candy store, for a box of chocolates for Nellie. To the butcher shop, for two chickens. I still had a couple dollars left, but headed home. I had traded or sold all my ties.

Nellie was really worried. I blew the horn when I reached our place and she came running out. I had picked up two of my bags that had doll heads popping out, hung the wreath on my arm and called her to help me. She took one look and started to cry. She assumed I had stolen all of these things. I explained how I had sold some ties and showed her the money, and traded others for these gifts for our best Christmas ever. I even had the chickens in the car for our Christmas dinner.

My Christmas Miracle

by

Taylor Caldwell

For many of us, one Christmas stands out from all the others, the one when the meaning of the day shone clearest.

Although I did not guess it, my own "truest" Christmas began on a rainy spring day in the bleakest year of my life. Recently divorced, I was in my twenties, had no job, and was on my way downtown to go the rounds of the employment offices. I had no umbrella, for my old one had fallen apart, and I could not afford another one. I sat down in the streetcar, and there against the seat was a beautiful silk umbrella with a silver handle inlaid with gold and flecks of bright enamel. I had never seen anything so lovely.

I examined the handle and saw a name engraved among the golden scrolls. The usual procedure would have been to turn in the umbrella to the conductor, but on impulse I decided to take it with me and find the owner myself. I got off the streetcar in a downpour and thankfully opened the umbrella to protect myself. Then I searched a telephone book for the name on the umbrella and found it. I called, and a lady answered.

Yes, she said in surprise, that was her umbrella, which her parents, now dead, had given her for a birthday present. But, she added, it had been stolen from her locker

---

at school (she was a teacher) more than a year before. She was so excited that I forgot I was looking for a job and went directly to her small house. She took the umbrella, and her eyes filled with tears.

The teacher wanted to give me a reward, but—though twenty dollars was all I had in the world—her happiness at retrieving this special possession was such that to have accepted money would have spoiled something. We talked for a while, and I must have given her my address. I don't remember.

The next six months were wretched. I was able to obtain only temporary employment here and there, for a small salary, though this was what they now call the Roaring Twenties. But I put aside twenty-five or fifty cents when I could afford it for my little girl's Christmas presents. (It took me six months to save eight dollars.) My last job ended the day before Christmas, my thirty dollar rent was soon due, and I had fifteen dollars to my name—which Peggy and I would need for food. She was home from her convent boarding school and was excitedly looking forward to her gifts the next day, which I had already purchased. I had bought her a small tree, and we were going to decorate it that night.

The stormy air was full of the sound of Christmas merriment as I walked from the streetcar to my small apartment. Bells rang and children shouted in the bitter dusk of the evening, and windows were lighted and everyone was running and laughing. But there would be no Christmas for me, I knew, no gifts, no remembrance whatsoever. As I struggled through the snowdrifts, I just about reached the lowest point in my life. Unless a miracle happened I would be homeless in January, foodless, jobless. I had prayed steadily for weeks, and there had been no answer but this coldness and darkness, this harsh air, this abandonment. God and men had completely forgotten me. I felt old as death, and as lonely. What was to become of us?

I looked in my mailbox. There were only bills in it, a sheaf of them, and two white envelopes which I was sure contained more bills. I went up three dusty flights of stairs, and I cried, shivering in my thin coat. But I made myself smile so I could greet my little daughter with a pretense of happiness. She opened the door for me and threw herself in my arms, screaming joyously and demanding that we decorate the tree immediately.

Peggy was not yet six years old and had been alone all day while I worked. She had set our kitchen table for our evening meal, proudly, and put pans out and the three cans of food which would be our dinner. For some reason, when I looked at those pans and cans, I felt broken-hearted. We would have only hamburgers for our Christmas dinner tomorrow, and gelatin. I stood in the cold little kitchen, and misery overwhelmed me. For the first time in my life, I doubted the existence of God and His mercy, and the coldness in my heart was colder than ice.

The doorbell rang, and Peggy ran fleetly to answer it, calling that it must be Santa Claus. Then I heard a man talking heartily to her and went to the door. He was a delivery man, and his arms were full of big parcels, and he was laughing at my child's frenzied joy and her dancing. "This is a mistake," I said, but he read the name on the parcels, and they were for me. When he had gone I could only stare at the boxes. Peggy and I sat on the floor and opened them. A huge doll, three times the size of the one I had bought for her, gloves, candy, a beautiful leather purse. Incredible! I looked for the name of the sender. It was the teacher, the address simply "California," where she had moved.

Our dinner that night was the most delicious I had

ever eaten. I could only pray to myself, "Thank you, Father." I forgot I had no money for the rent and only fifteen dollars in my purse and no job. My child and I ate and laughed together in happiness. Then we decorated the little tree and marveled at it. I put Peggy to bed and set up her gifts around the tree, and a sweet peace flooded me like a benediction. I had some hope again. I could even examine the sheaf of bills without cringing. Then I opened the two white envelopes. One contained a check for thirty dollars from a company I had worked for briefly in the summer. It was, said a note, my "Christmas bonus." My rent!

The other envelope was an offer of a permanent position with the government—to begin two days after Christmas. I sat with the letter in my hand and the check on the table before me, and I think that was the most joyful moment of my life up to that time.

The church bells began to ring. I hurriedly looked at my child, who was sleeping blissfully, and ran down to the street. Everywhere people were walking to church to celebrate the birth of the Saviour. People smiled at me and I smiled back. The storm had stopped, the sky was pure and glittering with stars.

"The Lord is born!" sang the bells to the crystal night and the laughing darkness. Someone began to sing, "Come, All Ye Faithful!" I joined in and sang with the strangers all about me.

I am not alone at all, I thought. I was never alone at all.

And that, of course, is the message of Christmas. We are never alone. Not when the night is darkest, the wind coldest, the world seemingly most indifferent. For this is still the time God chooses.

An Exchange of Gifts

by

Diane Rayner

I grew up believing that Christmas was a time when wise and royal visitors came riding, when at midnight the barnyard animals talked to one another, and in the light of a fabulous star, God came down to us as a little child. Christmas to me has always been a time of enchantment, and never more so than the year that my son Marty was eight.

That was the same year that my three children and I had moved into a cozy new trailer home in a forested area just outside of Redmond, Washington. As the holiday approached, our spirits were light, not to be dampened even by the winter rains that swept down Puget Sound to douse our home and make our floor muddy.

Throughout that December, Marty had been the most spirited, and busiest, of us all. He was my youngest—a cheerful boy, blond haired and playful, with a quaint habit of looking up at you and cocking his head like a puppy when you talked to him. Actually the reason for this was that Marty was deaf in his left ear, but it was a condition that he never complained about.

For weeks I'd been watching Marty. I knew that something was going on with him that he was not telling me about. I saw how eagerly he made his bed, took out the trash, and carefully set the table and helped Rick and Pam

---

prepare dinner before I got home from work. I saw how he silently collected his tiny allowance and tucked it away, spending not a cent of it. I had no idea what all this quiet activity was about, but I suspected that somehow it had something to do with Kenny.

Kenny was Marty's friend, and ever since they'd found each other in the springtime, they were seldom apart. If you called to one, you got them both. Their world was in the meadow, a horse pasture broken by a small winding stream, where the boys caught frogs and snakes, where they'd search for arrowheads or hidden treasure, or where they'd spend an afternoon feeding peanuts to the squirrels.

Times were hard for our little family, and we had to do some scrimping to get by. But Kenny's family was desperately poor, and his mother was having a real struggle feeding and clothing her two children. They were a good, solid family; but Kenny's mom was a proud woman, very proud, and she had strict rules.

How we worked, as we did each year, to make our home festive for the holiday! Our Christmas gifts were handcrafted and hidden away, and ornaments were strung about the place.

Marty and Kenny would sometimes sit still at the table long enough to help make cornucopias or weave little baskets for the tree; but then, in a flash, one would whisper to the other, and they would be out the door and into the horse pasture or sliding cautiously under the electric fence that separated our home from Kenny's.

One night shortly before Christmas—when my hands were deep in peppernoder dough, shaping tiny nutlike Danish cookies that were heavily spiced with cinnamon—Marty came into the kitchen and told me in a tone mixed with great pleasure and pride, "Mom, I've bought Kenny a Christmas present. Want to see it?"

So that's what he's been up to, I said to myself.

"It's something he's wanted for a long, long time, Mom," Marty said.

After carefully wiping his hands on a dish towel, he pulled from his pocket a small box. Lifting the lid, I gazed at the pocket compass that my son had been saving all those allowances to buy. A little compass to point an eight-year-old adventurer through the woods.

"It's a lovely gift, Martin," I said, but even as I spoke, a disturbing thought came to my mind. Kenny's family could barely afford to exchange gifts among themselves, and giving presents to others was out of the question. I was sure that Kenny's proud mother would not permit her son to receive something he could not return in kind.

Gently, carefully, I talked over the problem with Marty. He understood what I was saying.

"I know, Mom, I know...but what if it was a secret? What if they never found out who gave it?"

I didn't know how to answer him. I just didn't know. And so the matter was left up in the air.

The day before Christmas was rainy, cold, and gray. The three kids and I all but fell over one another as we put finishing touches on Christmas secrets and prepared for family and friends who would be dropping by.

Night settled in. The rain continued. I looked out the window over the sink and felt an odd sadness. How mundane the rain seemed for a Christmas Eve. Would wise men and kings come riding on such a night? I doubted it. It seemed to me that strange and wonderful things happened only on clear nights, nights when one could at least see a star in the heavens.

I turned from the window, and as I checked on the ham and homemade bread in the oven, I saw Marty slip out the door. He wore his coat over his pajamas. I knew he was clutching a tiny, colorfully wrapped box in his pocket.

Later he told me what happened to him that night. Down through the soggy pasture he'd gone, then a quick slide under the electric fence and across the yard to Kenny's house. Up the steps on tiptoes, shoes squishing; opening the screen door just a crack; the gift placed on the doorstep; then a deep breath, a reach for the doorbell, and a press on it—hard.

Quickly Marty turned, ran down the steps and across the yard in a wild race to get away unnoticed. Then, suddenly, he banged into the electric fence.

The shock sent him reeling. He lay stunned on the wet ground. His body tingled and he gasped for breath. Then slowly, weakly, confused, and frightened, he struggled back home.

"Marty," we cried as he stumbled through the door, "what happened?" His lower lip quivered, his eyes brimmed with tears.

"I forgot about the fence, and it knocked me down!"

I hugged his muddy little body to me. He was still dazed, and there was a red mark from the fence beginning to blister on his face from his mouth to his ear. Quickly I treated the blister, and with a warm cup of cocoa soothing him, Marty's bright spirits returned. I tucked him into bed, and just before he fell asleep he looked up at me and said, "Mom, I'm sure Kenny didn't see me."

That Christmas Eve I went to bed unhappy and puzzled. The encounter with the electric fence seemed such a cruel thing to happen to a little boy while on the purest kind of Christmas mission, doing what the Lord wants us all to do, giving to others, and giving in secret at that. I did not sleep well that night. Somewhere deep inside I think I must have been feeling the disappointment that the night of Christmas had come and it had been just an ordinary problem-filled night—no mysterious enhancement at all.

But I was wrong.

By morning the rain had stopped and the sun shone. The streak on Marty's face was very red, but I could tell that the burn was not serious. We opened our presents, and soon, not unexpectedly, Kenny was knocking on the door, eager to show Marty his new compass and tell about the mystery of its arrival. It was plain that Kenny didn't suspect Marty at all, and while the two of them talked, Marty just smiled and smiled.

Then I noticed that while the two boys were comparing their Christmases, nodding and gesturing and chattering away, Marty was not cocking his head. When Kenny was talking, Marty was listening with his deaf ear—the ear that had slammed into the fence.

Weeks later a report came from the school nurse verifying what Marty and I already knew: "Marty now has complete hearing in both ears."

The mystery of how Marty regained his hearing, and still has it, remains just that—a mystery. Doctors suspect, of course, that the shock from the electric fence was somehow responsible. Perhaps so. Whatever the reason, I just remain thankful to God for the good exchange of gifts made that night.

So you see, strange and wonderful things still happen on the night of our Lord's birth. And one does not have to have a clear night, either, to follow a fabulous star.

IV

And On Earth Peace

As a child living in Idaho during World War II, I remember a prisoner of war camp for captured German soldiers outside of town. One snowy afternoon when our family was driving through the countryside, we saw the POWs out walking in formation, guarded by soldiers with rifles. I said how awful it would be to be a prisoner in the winter, half-way around the world from home. My mother replied, "Don't feel sorry for them! They give them chocolates!"

I was surprised to realize that so many of my best stories are from wartime. It is as if the worst of times can bring out the best in good people. When I asked the Englishman who wrote "Christmas Day, Italy, 1943" for permission to share his story, he graciously agreed, explaining, "It is one of the great experiences of my life."

As war's alarms inexorably work to deprive men of their humanity, they must fight their greatest battle—the battle to maintain human decency in the midst of turmoil. At Christmas time we are buoyed up by the hopeful message of the angels who announced of Christ's birth: "Glory to God in the highest, and on earth peace, good will toward men." (Luke 2: 14)

Christmas Eve in the Stable

by

David Niven

My most memorable contribution to Christmas—if I can call it that—and indeed my only conscious effort in this direction happened on Christmas Day in 1939.

I had just arrived from Hollywood to volunteer for the British Army. Having had some previous military experience, I was commissioned a second lieutenant and given command of a platoon. We were about to be sent to France and no one was very happy about it. Most of the men had been conscripted from good civilian jobs; this was the "phoney war" period before the big German attack of the following spring and it all seemed a ridiculous waste of time to most of them. Being commanded by a Hollywood movie star was an additional irritant for them and made the whole thing seem even more ridiculous. The men were not mutinous—but they were certainly forty of the least well-disposed characters I have ever been associated with, let alone been in command of.

We were not permitted liberty on that Christmas Eve because we were due to leave England and our families the next day—a fine prospect for the holidays. The entire platoon was billeted in the shabby stables of a farm near Dover. Each man gathered up what little straw he could find for bedding.

"Christmas Eve in the Stable" by David Niven. Published in *Christmas with Ed Sullivan*, written and compiled by Ed Sullivan, published in 1959 by The McGraw-Hill Companies. Reprinted by permission of The McGraw-Hill Company.

I could sense that everyone disliked me intensely. The air was thick with sarcastic cracks about my motion-picture bravery in "The Charge of the Light Brigade," "The Dawn Patrol," and "The Prisoner of Zenda."

It so happens that every night of my life I have knelt down by my bed and said a few simple prayers—I am ashamed to say that in general these prayers, if heeded, would aid my personal well-being to no end. Nevertheless they were prayers of a sort—to God.

I was faced with a difficult decision. If I suddenly knelt in prayer, the chances were that forty tough soldiers would take it as a final evidence of Hollywood flamboyance.

On the other hand, I have always felt that prayers said in comfortable and unobtrusive positions don't really count.

Finally I plucked up my courage. I knelt and said my prayers.

As I prayed, the snickering and the laughter slowly died away.

I suppose the exciting end of this story would be that some vast, hulking conscript kicked me over, whereupon I fought valiantly and victoriously for the sake of our Lord.

The true ending was far more satisfactory.

When I finished my prayers and lay down again on the straw, I looked rather sheepishly around the stable and saw at least a dozen soldiers kneeling quietly and praying in their own way.

A Christmas Ballad for the Captain

by
William J. Lederer

Many years ago, when my three children were still quite young, they asked the inevitable question about Santa Claus. Like most parents, I reassured them, but when asked for proof, became evasive.

Determined to uncover some convincing evidence, I dug back into my memory for every experience I'd ever had with the reality of what is called Santa. Finally, I returned to my children with this true story of an event that took place during the early months of World War II, when I was an officer on a Navy destroyer. I did not write this story. It was written by one of the crewmen shortly after our ship was torpedoed on the way back from Anzio. His reason for writing it was to send it to all surviving crew members as a small Christmas present.

Perhaps it does not reveal the answer to the question about Santa. But it does concern one man's discovery of the joy of giving—which is, after all, what Christmas is really all about. Captain Elias Stark, commanding officer of our destroyer, was a square-shouldered New Hampshire man, as quiet and austere as the granite mountains of his native state. About the only time the enlisted men heard him talk was when they first reported aboard. He would invite them to his cabin for a one-minute speech of welcome, then question them about their

---

families and note the names and addresses of the sailors' next of kin.

That was the way he had first met the "Unholy Ks"—Krakow, Kratch, Koenig and Kelly. They had arrived from the naval prison at Portsmouth, New Hampshire. Most of the prison group were bad eggs, but the worst were these four sailors from a small coal-mining town in Pennsylvania. They had chests and shoulders like buffaloes, fists like sledgehammers, black stubble beards, and manners to match. They had once been good kids, the mainstays of St. Stephen's choir, but somehow they had gone astray. They seemed to specialize in getting into trouble together. All four went into the Navy directly from reform school. Within six months, they were in serious trouble again and had been sent to Portsmouth Naval Prison.

When they were called to the captain's cabin, they listened to his speech with exaggerated expressions of boredom. Then the Old Man broke out his record book to note the names and addresses of their next of kin. He looked up inquiringly.

Krakow, the leader, took the initiative. Spreading his tremendous arms, he pulled Kelly, Kratch and Koenig into a tight circle. "The four of us, sir, ain't got no family. We ain't got parents or wives or relatives." He paused. "All we got is girlfriends, eh, fellas?"

Captain Stark simply puffed on his pipe. Patiently he asked, "Would you give me your best ladies' names and addresses for our records?"

The Unholy Ks glanced at one another.

Krakow said, "Sir, we don't feel like it's an officer's business who our girls are." He stopped as Kelly tugged his sleeve and whispered to him.

"Okay," continued Krakow sarcastically, "you want to know who our best girls are, I'll tell you. Mine's Rita

Hayworth, Kelly's is Ginger Rogers, Kratch's is Lana Turner and Koenig's is Paulette Goddard. They all got the same address: Hollywood, sir."

"Very well," said the captain, "I will list those names in my records. Thank you, that will be all."

As soon as the Unholy Ks got below deck, they began bragging how they had made a fool out of the Old Man. But actually the captain had a good reason for obtaining personal information about the men. He strongly believed it was his duty to keep their families informed on how they were getting along. So, once every three months, in blunt New England fashion, he sent a personal note written in a tiny, neat hand to everyone's next of kin.

In September, after a year in the combat zone, our destroyer went to the Brooklyn Navy Yard for a three-week overhaul. Almost all the officers and men went home on furloughs. Only the Old Man stayed on board the entire time, working alone, day and night. No one knew the nature of his apparently urgent business; but whenever we passed his cabin we saw him hunched over his desk, scratching away with an old-fashioned pen.

We were puzzled also by the scores of parcels in plain wrappers that began coming to the Old Man before we sailed. It was not until much later that we would find out what they contained.

Afterward, our destroyer went to sea again, protecting convoys across the North Atlantic to England. It was rough work. Icy gales battered us; ships were torpedoed almost every night. We had little sleep and much physical discomfort. Everyone drooped with fatigue. Tempers became edgy, and there were fights. Captain Stark was constantly on the bridge, smoking his pipe and watching everything carefully.

If he knew how the Unholy Ks were trying to destroy the ship's morale, he never mentioned it. It was their well-rendered ballads that did the dirty work. Everyone was afraid of these four bullies, but when they sang insidious songs about the ship's officers, the crew listened. Their lyrics were so catchy that a song rendered in the washroom would be repeated all over the ship within a half-hour. No officers ever heard the four men sing; but the results of their music were uncomfortably apparent.

The Unholy Ks had one song about the hundreds of packages the captain had locked in the forward peak tank. The lyrics said that the boxes contained silk stockings, cigarettes, whiskey and other black-market goods the captain was going to sell in England. They depicted the captain becoming a millionaire and retiring to a mansion in New Hampshire as soon as the war was over.

The crew began to ask questions: Why should the Old Man be hiding the parcels? Why had they been delivered with so much secrecy? It was even rumored that the Old Man was head of a black-market cartel and the cartons contained drugs stolen from Navy supply depots. But when the crew saw Captain Stark, tall, quiet, dignified, they knew in their hearts that the rumors were impossible.

In mid-December, we shoved off from Newfoundland with another convoy; there were 62 ships in the group. Almost immediately we ran into a gale. The ships wallowed and floundered among mountainous waves. For nearly a week we had nothing to eat but sandwiches, and it was impossible to sleep. On top of this misery, we received an emergency alert and intelligence that the largest Nazi submarine wolf pack ever assembled was shadowing our convoy.

After a few days at sea, all grumbling and grousing stopped. We were too weary to do anything but stand watch, straining our eyes and ears for the enemy. Finally the storm slackened and the submarines closed in. During the beginning of the second week, hardly a night went by without the sky lighting up with the explosions of torpedoed ships.

Then, at sunrise on the 25th of December, as we neared the southwest tip of Ireland, our protection arrived—Royal Navy planes. The seas calmed and we relaxed; for the first time in what had seemed ages, the men were able to get a hot meal and sleep. All hands, except those on watch, turned in thankfully, exhausted.

Suddenly at 9 o'clock on this Christmas morning, the bosun's mate piped reveille. A wave of grumbling passed over the ship. We had all expected to be able to sleep in unless there was an attack. A few minutes later, Captain Stark's voice came over the loudspeaker. "This is the captain speaking. Shipmates, I know you are tired and want to sleep. But today is Christmas. There are special surprise packages from your families. They have been unloaded from the forward peak tanks and have been distributed throughout the ship alphabetically."

The news exploded through the ship. Men scrambled for their packages. Sailors sat all over the decks, cutting string, tearing paper, wiping away tears and shouting to shipmates about what they had received.

But the four Unholy Ks found no presents. They stood together, watching the others sullenly.

"Christmas!" said Koenig. "It's only an excuse to get suckers to spend money."

"Don't show me your new wristwatch," sneered Krakow to a young sailor who proudly held it up. "If I need a new ticker, I'll buy me one."

One happy kid came jiggling up with a huge box of fudge. "From my girl," he sang out, "Now I see why the Old Man wanted her name and address."

"Hey!" said Krakow, grabbing Kelly's arm. "Didn't we give the Old Man our girls' names and addresses?"

"Yeah," said Kratch, beginning to grin slyly. "Rita Hayworth, Ginger Rogers, Lana Turner and Paulette Goddard."

"Then how come we didn't get anything?"

"Let's go see the Old Man."

The Unholy Ks, smiling evilly, went to the captain's cabin.

"Captain Stark, sir," said Krakow with mock respect, "we got a complaint. Everybody on this ship got presents from the names and addresses they gave you."

The captain looked at the four men gravely. "Don't you think that's nice?"

"But we gave you names and addresses, and we didn't get no presents."

"Oh, you didn't?" said the Old Man slowly.

"No sir, everyone but us. That's discrimination, sir."

"By gum," said the captain standing up, "there are four extra packages. Now I just wonder...." He went to his bunk and pulled a blanket off a pile of parcels.

"There's one for me!" hollered Kelly, surging forward.

Captain Stark stood up to his full six feet and blocked the way. Reaching into the bunk, he handed out the packages to the four men, one at a time.

"Now, if you'll excuse me, I'll conduct Yuletide services." He went out to the bridge.

The Unholy Ks ripped the colored wrappings. Krakow couldn't open his fast enough and took his knife to slash the ribbon. Inside the fancy box was a pair of knitted woolen gloves. He tried them on his big red hands.

"Gee, the right size!"

There was something else in the box. It was a picture of a shapely woman in a low-cut dress; and there was writing on it.

Dear Joe Krakow,

I knitted these gloves especially for you because you are my best boyfriend in the U.S. Navy. I hope that they'll keep you warm and that you'll have a wonderful Christmas wherever you may be.

From your best pal, Rita Hayworth.

Joe Krakow felt around his pockets for a handkerchief but couldn't find one. "What did you guys get?" he said, sniffling.

"Me?" said Koenig shrilly, "I got a wallet and a picture of Paulette Goddard! From Paulette Goddard!"

Kelly received a watch and an autographed picture from Ginger Rogers; and Kratch's present from Lana Turner was a gold fountain pen and a sentimentally inscribed photograph.

The Unholy Ks shuffled to the bridge, where Captain Stark, his Bible open, stood in front of the microphone.

Krakow said, "Captain, sir...."

"Later," the captain replied bluntly, without even turning. He switched on the loudspeaker, announced church services and read the story of the Nativity to all hands. Below, in the engine room, men listened, and in the chiefs' quarters, in the galley, in the mess compartments—throughout the ship, 250 sailors listened as the Old Man read the story of Jesus.

When he finished, he said he hoped everyone would join him in singing a few carols.

The Unholy Ks pushed in on the captain. "Let us help you, sir," said Krakow urgently.

"This is not your type of song," the captain replied.

"Please, sir, the least we can do is lead the singing."

"Please, sir, let this be our Christmas present to you."

"A Christmas present for me?" mused the Old Man. "Why, yes, we'd all appreciate having a choir for the occasion. What shall we start with?"

The four sailors looked at the Old Man and then down at the photographs and presents clutched tightly under their arms. They gathered around the microphone. Krakow coughed; then in his deep bass he boomed, "Shipmates, this is Koenig, Kelly, Kratch and me, Krakow—four no-good bums. Today is Christmas, and we want to sing you a special ballad." He paused, and wiped his eyes and nose on his shirtsleeve.

Krakow raised his hand like a symphony conductor, and the quartet began to sing:

Silent night, holy night,
All is calm, all is bright....

The magic of the holy music spread. Everyone on the ship joined in. Even Captain Elias Stark, the granite man from New Hampshire, moved into the quartet, inclined his head and, in reedy tenor, swelled the song.

Sleep in heavenly peace,
Sleep in heavenly peace.

The joyous music rose above the noise of the ocean and the destroyer's engines. During the third stanza, an enormous bird soared in from the lowhanging clouds and landed in the after rigging. It flapped its great wings and made noises as if it, too, were singing our Christmas ballad along with us. My shipmates said it was an albatross. But, even though my eyes were filled with tears, I'd swear that it was an angel.

Of course, that was many years ago when I was still a kid. But even then I could recognize an angel when I saw one. As sure as my name's Joe Krakow.

Christmas Day, Italy, 1943

by

Walter Stevenson

I have never seen the spirit of Christmas so profoundly manifested in such unlikely circumstances as I did on Christmas Day, 1943.

I was in a British division that was part of the American Fifth Army in Italy. Casualties had been continuous and heavy since we had landed at Salerno. By December, we were advancing slowly north of Naples—cold, very wet, very muddy, quite weary, and a little homesick. Never had the prospect of Christmas seemed so bleak and far away.

Taking advantage of a lull in the fighting, we decided to take up position on a small farm. The countryside was deserted, so we were surprised as we opened the farmhouse door to find a farmer and his wife and seven children. They invited us to join them for evening soup.

God had protected them, the farmer told us. The young children, ranging from 2 to 14, had been huddled in the cellar for days. Two girls had sores on their legs, another had been hit in the back by a piece of shrapnel, and the father's arm was injured. Most of the cattle had been killed, the barn had been burned, and the retreating Germans had taken their horses, most of their food, and some of their household items. They had no soap, no medical supplies, and very little food, but the house was

---

sound, they were together as a family, and they didn't want to move.

With their cooperation, we set up a command post in their house. I was a medical orderly, so our commanding officer told me to do what I could for the children. The entire battery was concerned for this family, whose Christmas prospects seemed bleak indeed.

Without telling them, we collected precious bars of toilet soap, talcum powder, candy, and various odds and ends for the children and their parents. We found a small tree that had been uprooted; it was not a traditional Christmas tree, but we decorated it with silver paper, colored wrappers, and cordite bags. When we had finished, it was the best Christmas tree we had ever seen, decorated with all the love those soldiers wanted to lavish on their own families. At bedtime on Christmas Eve, we could hear the children praying for the English soldiers and their families.

When we presented our gifts to the parents early Christmas morning, they wept with joy. That Christmas dinner was the first time any of us had spaghetti for Christmas and the first time the Italians had eaten English Christmas pudding. I will never forget the children's delight over such simple presents, and the hugs and kisses that brought tears to every eye. The family couldn't speak English, and most of us spoke very little Italian, but we all understood that farmer's toast: "If the spirit that is here now could be in the hearts of all men, this war would never have happened." For some of those soldiers, it was their last Christmas on earth, and for those of us who survived, it was certainly the most memorable.

The Creche

by

Glenn Kittler

During World War II, I was stationed on a South Pacific island. Although Christmas was approaching, the nighttime temperature rarely fell below 80 degrees. We swam almost every day, and wildflowers and flamboyant trees were in brilliant blossom. To add to this, the tragedy of the war made it difficult for us to feel the least Christmas spirit.

But then a big box arrived from home. In it my mother had sent all the figurines for a creche: Mother and Child, Joseph, the shepherds, angels, the animals, each carefully packed in sawdust and wood shavings.

Immediately I took the box over to the makeshift chapel we had built from scraps. The chaplain and a couple of my buddies were there, and together we built a stage-like box of plywood, scorching it and varnishing it, then installing a tiny lighting system. On Christmas Eve we collected some straw and wildflowers and small branches for the interior of the box. Then we set the figurines in place, just as we had so often seen them back home. When the men–Americans of almost every faith and creed–arrived for Christmas Eve services, you should have seen the joy and wonder that lit up their eyes.

Was it Christmas? Yes, it certainly was. Our creche

---

was a sturdy symbol of God's reaching out into a strange and dangerous place. Just as His presence was with the Christ Child in Bethlehem long ago, so it was there in our hearts in the South Pacific.

Christmas in the Trenches

from the album

John McCutcheon: Live at Wolftrap

by John McCutcheon

There are some songs as a writer that you write and other songs that you just sort of write down. They come through you and that was definitely the case with this song, so I can speak about it with a certain amount of distance. This came to me totally as a gift. In a five-minute span it was there and some of the most remarkable things that have happened to me in my life have happened to me because of this song.

Probably the most remarkable thing that happened to me was a couple of years ago when I was at a festival in Denmark—a little town called Turndur. Every time I played, there was a little bevy of very old—and we are talking *old*—German men who'd come across the border and show up at my shows. They usually came in late, came trotting up the aisle and there usually wasn't a seat left. So they just stood there at the edge of the stage, watched me without expression, and turned around and left when I was done.

During the last set, I was watching these guys turn around to leave as I finished my last song. I was thinking, "Who are these guys?" So I set down my autoharp or

---

"Christmas in the Trenches" from the album *John McCutcheon Live at Wolf Trap*. (Rounder Records) available from Appalseed Productions, 1025 Locust VA. Charlottesville, VA 22901. (c) 1990 by John McCutcheon/Appalsongs (ASCAP). Used by permission.

whatever I was playing, jumped off the edge of the stage and ran up the aisle and caught the last guy. I said, "You guys have been real sweet showing up all these places, but what's the deal?"

One guy said, "We are here because of that song."

I said, "What song?"

"Well, you know, that song that is on the radio. That's how we heard about you and this festival. Because all our lives, our families and friends have told us that we are crazy—couldn't possibly have happened to us—but then we heard your song on the radio and said, 'See! See. Because we were there.'" And they were there seventy-five years ago, that Christmas Eve when the events that this song commemorates happened.

> Oh, my name is Francis Tolliver, I come from Liverpool.
> Two years ago the war was waiting for me after school.
> From Belgium and to Flanders, to Germany, to here,
> I fought for King and Country I love dear.
>
> This Christmas in the trenches where the frost so bitter hung,
> The frozen fields of France were still; no Christmas songs were sung.
> Our families back in England were toasting us that day,
> Their brave and glorious lads so far away.
>
> Well, I was lying with my messmates on a cold and rocky ground
> When across the lines of battle came a most peculiar sound.

Says I, "Now listen up me boys." Each soldier strained to hear
As one young German voice sang out so clear.

"He's singing bloody well you know," my partner says to me.
Soon one by one each German voice joined in in harmony.
The cannons rested silently and the gas clouds rolled no more,
As Christmas brought us respite from the war.

As soon as they were finished and a reverent pause was spent,
"God Rest You Merry Gentlemen" struck up some lads from Kent.
Oh, the next one they sang was "Stillenacht" ("Tis 'Silent Night'," says I)
And in two tongues one song filled up that sky.

"Someone's coming towards us," the front line sentry cried.
All sights were fixed on one lone figure trudging from their side.
The truce flag like a Christmas star shone on that plain so bright
As he bravely strolled unarmed into the night.

Soon one by one on either side walked into no-man's land.
With neither gun nor bayonet we met there hand to hand.
We shared some secret brandy and we wished each other well,
And in a flare-lit soccer game we gave them hell.

We traded chocolates, cigarettes and photographs from home;
These sons and fathers far away from families of their own.
Young Sanders played his squeeze-box and they had a violin,
This curious and unlikely band of men.

Soon daylight stole upon us and France was France once more.
With sad farewells we each began to settle back to war.
But the question haunted every heart that beat that wondrous night,
"Whose family have I fixed within my sights?"

'Twas Christmas in the trenches where the frost so bitter hung
The frozen hills of France were warmed as songs of peace were sung;
The walls they kept between us to exact the work of war
Had been crumbled and were gone forever more.

Oh, my name is Frances Tolliver, in Liverpool I dwell.
Each Christmas come since World War I, I've learned these lessons well.
That the ones who call the shots won't be among the dead and lame
And on each end of the rifle we're the same.

POW Camp Brings Yule Meaning

by
Harold Kinsch

The meanings and messages of Christmas are as numerous and varied as lights and tinsel on a Christmas tree. But like the tree-top star or angel, the uppermost significance of this most blessed of days lies in giving and in that most precious gift which is love.

Apart from the paper- and foil-wrapped presents that we exchange and endow on our children each Christmas, there are gifts which come to us in wonderfully strange and sometimes hidden ways.

Which brings to mind a special gift of understanding which came to me when I was a lad of seven or eight one bleak Christmas during the depths of World War II.

Earlier that year, the U.S. military command constructed a compound for German prisoners of war just outside my small rural hometown in north central Iowa.

Naturally the townspeople were resentful of this unwanted intrusion by the hated enemy, Hitler's Nazi troops which were inflicting terrible casualties on Allied forces. Here and there around town, gold stars hung in windows, reminding all that for many families this Christmas would be a time of sadness.

The fear and hatred against the enemy soldiers in our midst seemed to further diminish the already war-weary Christmas spirit of my hometown. Influenced by

---

the attitudes of adults and by the anti-German propaganda constantly spewed out by the press and radio, I too was caught up in the acerbity against our foreign guests.

Then one day several weeks before Christmas, a story appeared in our local weekly paper about a wondrous nativity scene that had been constructed in the camp by the German POWs. My family and I were incredulous. Was it possible that a group of hard-bitten troops from the Third Reich—portrayed by the propaganda machine as ruthless murderers—could have created a work of love and beauty?

The public was invited to view the prisoners' handiwork and at the earliest opportunity we went out to the camp. Our curiosity was apparently shared by others because when we arrived there was a long line of onlookers waiting to get inside the building where the display had been constructed.

I'll never forget the awesome feeling that swept over me as I followed my parents, brothers and sisters through the exhibit area. It was truly magnificent. Occupying most of the building, the scene reenacted with lifesize figures and realistic settings the story of Christ's birth.

Each statue—Mary, Joseph, the Infant Jesus, the Wise Men, Shepherds—was a work of art, created by obviously talented European artisans. But the scene seemed to glow with an aura of reverence and tenderness which could only come from loving hands even though those hands once cradled rifles and grasped bayonets.

Perhaps the greatest impression left on my young mind came from the prisoners themselves. It was the first time I had seen German soldiers face-to-face. Unlike the brutal stereotype of the jack-booted Nazi troopers prevalent at the time, these men seemed warm, friendly and utterly human.

Now I could understand what had been very difficult—nearly impossible—to reconcile earlier. That our enemies were ordinary human beings, like my family and neighbors, possessed of the same fears, feelings, compassion and beliefs.

The war dragged on and newspaper and radio accounts of the battles continuously brought home its reality. But I had faith that one day it would end and there would be peace. When peace finally came, forgiveness and understanding of those who once fought against my cousins and neighbors—and of mankind in general—was far easier because of the special gift that came one Christmas at a snowy POW camp in northern Iowa.

Have a Merry Christmas.

V

'Twas the Night Before Christmas

Some writers have told such wonderful Christmas stories that their works are a part of our culture's holiday tradition. Two of the best are Charles Dickens' "A Christmas Carol" and a story best known now as a song, "Rudolph, the Red-Nosed Reindeer." But how did Charles Dickens and Robert L. May come to write these tales?

I have found as much inspiration in these stories behind the stories as in the stories themselves. And, because it is hard to find, I give you the original text of "Rudolph the Red-Nosed Reindeer," first published as a holiday give-away book in 1936 by Montgomery Ward Company, for whom writer May worked. I remember my parents bringing this newsprint booklet home after a Christmas shopping trip. My sibs and I were delighted!

I couldn't have included "Rudolph" without a miracle of my own. In seeking permission to publish the original story, I hit the proverbial brick wall at every turn. No one knew where to find the publisher or family member who owned the copyright. Then, one evening as I was chatting with a neighbor at a bridal shower, she asked me what I'd been doing lately. For some reason, I told her about this book, and about the search for "Rudolph." "I have a hardback copy of that!" she said.

"So do I," I told her. "Thanks anyway." She brought her book over just the same. Both of our books were garage sale finds—but hers was in better condition, with a dust jacket. The dust jacket told me that Robert May's papers were at Dartmouth University. Several phone calls later, I was able to speak to one of May's daughters. And Barbara May Lewis generously agreed to tell me how Rudolph came to be.

The Second Greatest Christmas Story Ever Told

by
Thomas J. Burns

On an early October evening in 1843, Charles Dickens stepped from the brick-and-stone portico of his home near Regent's Park in London. The cool air of dusk was a relief from the day's unseasonal humidity, as the author began his nightly walk through what he called "the black streets" of the city.

A handsome man with flowing brown hair and normally sparkling eyes, Dickens was deeply troubled. The thirty-one-year-old father of four had thought he was at the peak of his career. The *Pickwick Papers, Oliver Twist* and *Nicholas Nickleby* had all been popular; and *Martin Chuzzlewit*, which he considered his finest novel yet, was being published in monthly installments. But now, the celebrated writer was facing serious financial problems.

Some months earlier, his publisher had revealed that sales of the new novel were not what had been expected, and it might be necessary to sharply reduce Dickens' monthly advances against future sales.

The news had stunned the author. It seemed that his talent was being questioned. Memories of his childhood poverty resurfaced. Dickens was supporting a large, ex-

---

"The Second Greatest Christmas Story Ever Told" by Thomas J. Burns. Reprinted with permission from December 1989 *Reader's Digest*.

tended family, and his expenses were already nearly more than he could handle. His father and brothers were pleading for loans. His wife, Kate, was expecting their fifth child.

All summer long, Dickens worried about his mounting bills, especially the large mortgage that he owed on his house. He spent time at a seaside resort, where he had trouble sleeping and walked the cliffs for hours. He knew that he needed an idea that would earn him a large sum of money, and he needed the idea quickly. But in his depression, Dickens was finding it difficult to write. After returning to London, he hoped that resuming his nightly walks would help spark his imagination.

The yellow glow from the flickering gas lamps lit his way through London's better neighborhoods. Then gradually, as he neared the Thames River, only the dull light from tenement windows illuminated the streets, now litter-strewn and lined with open sewers. The elegant ladies and well-dressed gentlemen of Dickens' neighborhood were replaced by bawdy streetwalkers, pickpockets, footpads and beggars.

The dismal scene reminded him of the nightmare that often troubled his sleep: *A twelve-year old boy sits at a worktable piled high with pots of black boot paste. For twelve hours a day, six days a week, he attaches labels on the endless stream of pots to earn the six shillings that will keep him alive.*

The boy in the dream looks through the rotting warehouse floor into the cellar, where swarms of rats scurry about. Then he raises his eyes to the dirt-streaked window, dripping with condensation from London's wintry weather. The light is fading now, along with the boy's young hopes. His father is in debtor's prison, and the youngster is receiving only an hour of school lessons during his dinner break at the warehouse. He feels helpless, abandoned. There may never be celebration, joy or hope again....

This was no scene from the author's imagination. It was a period from his early life. Fortunately, Dickens' father had inherited some money, enabling him to pay off his debts and get out of prison—and his young son escaped a dreary fate.

Now the fear of being unable to pay his own debts haunted Dickens. Wearily, he started home from his long walk, no closer to an idea for the "cheerful, glowing" tale he wanted to tell than he'd been when he started out.

However, as he neared home, he felt a sudden flash of inspiration. What about a Christmas story! He would write one for the very people he passed on the black streets of London. People who lived and struggled with the same fears and longings he had known, people who hungered for a bit of cheer and hope.

But Christmas was less than three months away! How could he manage so great a task in so brief a time? The book would have to be short, certainly not a full novel. It would have to be finished by the end of November to be printed and distributed in time for Christmas sales. For speed, he struck on the idea of adapting a Christmas-goblin story from a chapter in The Pickwick Papers.

He would fill the story with the scenes and characters his readers loved. There would be a small, sickly child; his honest but ineffectual father; and, at the center of the piece, a selfish villain, an old man with a pointed nose and shriveled cheeks.

As the mild days of October gave way to a cool November, the manuscript grew, page by page, and the story took life. The basic plot was simple enough for children to understand, but evoked themes that would conjure up warm memories and emotions in an adult's heart: *After retiring alone to his cold, barren apartment on Christmas Eve, Ebeneezer Scrooge, a miserly London businessman, is visited by the spirit of his dead partner, Jacob Marley. Doomed by his greed and insensitivity to his fellow man when alive, Marley's ghost wanders the world in chains forged of his own indifference. He warns Scrooge that he must change, or suffer the same fate. The ghosts of Christmas Past, Christmas Present and Christmas Yet to Come appear and show Scrooge poignant scenes from his life and what will occur if he doesn't mend his ways. Filled with remorse, Scrooge renounces his former selfishness and becomes a kind, generous, loving person who has learned the true spirit of Christmas.*

Gradually, in the course of his writing, something surprising happened to Dickens. What had begun as a desperate, calculated plan to rescue himself from debt—"a little scheme," as he described it—soon began to work a change in the author. As he wrote about the kind of Christmas he loved—joyous family parties with clusters of mistletoe hanging from the ceiling; cheerful carols, games, dances and gifts; delicious feasts of roast goose, plum pudding, fresh breads, all enjoyed in front of a blazing yule log—the joy of the season he cherished began to alleviate his depression.

A Christmas Carol captured his heart and soul. It became a labor of love. Every time he dipped his quill pen into his ink, the characters seemed magically to take life: Tiny Tim with his crutches, Scrooge cowering in fear before the ghosts, Bob Cratchit drinking Christmas cheer in the face of poverty.

Each morning, Dickens grew excited and impatient to begin the day's work. "I was very much affected by the little book," he later wrote a newspaperman, and was "reluctant to lay it aside for a moment." A friend and Dickens' future biographer, John Forster, took note of the "strange mastery" the story held over the author. Dickens told a professor in America how, when writing, he "wept, and laughed and wept again." Dickens even took charge of the design of the book, deciding on a gold-stamped cover, a red-and-green title page with colored end papers, and four hand-colored etchings and four engraved woodcuts. To make the book affordable to the widest audience possible, he priced it at only five shillings.

At last, on December 2, he was finished, and the manuscript went to the printers. On December 17, the author's copies were delivered and Dickens was delighted. He had never doubted that *A Christmas Carol* would be popular. But neither he nor his publisher was ready for the overwhelming response that came. The first edition of six thousand copies sold out by Christmas Eve, and as the little book's heartwarming message spread, Dickens later recalled, he received "by every post, all manner of strangers writing all manner of letters about their homes and hearths, and how the *Carol* is read aloud there, and kept on a very little shelf by itself." Novelist William Makepeace Thackeray said of the *Carol*: "It seems to me a national benefit, and to every man or woman who reads it a personal kindness."

Despite the book's public acclaim, it did not turn into the immediate financial success that Dickens had hoped for, because of the quality production he demanded and the low price he placed on the book. Nevertheless, he made enough money from it to scrape by, and *A Christmas Carol's* enormous popularity revived his audience for subsequent novels, while giving a fresh, new direction to his life and career.

Although Dickens would write many other well-received and financially profitable books—*David*

Copperfield, A Tale of Two Cities, Great Expectations—nothing would ever quite equal the soul-satisfying joy he derived from his universally loved little novel. In time, some would call him the Apostle of Christmas. And, at his death in 1870, a poor child in London was heard to ask: "Dickens dead? Then will Father Christmas die too?"

In a very real sense, Dickens popularized many aspects of the Christmas we celebrate today, including great family gatherings, seasonal drinks and dishes and gift giving. Even our language has been enriched by the tale. Who has not known a "Scrooge" or uttered "Bah! Humbug!" when feeling irritated or disbelieving. And the phrase "Merry Christmas!" gained wider usage after the story appeared.

In the midst of self-doubt and confusion, a man sometimes does his best work. From the storm of tribulation comes a gift. For Charles Dickens, a little Christmas novel brought new-found faith in himself and in the redemptive joy of the season.

Memories of Rudolph

by

Barbara May Lewis*

It's 1939. I'm four years old. My father is a copywriter for Montgomery Ward. He writes the sketches when someone retires or is promoted. He writes the little ad-hoc pieces for special occasions. And this year he is asked to write a Christmas story as a giveaway for the toy department. That is Rudolph's genesis.

My father tried the story out on me. I remember that I didn't like the word "stomach" so he changed it to "tummy." He wanted to make sure it sat right with me, that I understood all the words and that they were the right words for my age group.

Dad was a great story teller, really magical! My favorite story of his was about a little girl who ran away from home and hid among the dolls in the department store. Somebody bought her and she had many adventures. After my mother died, Dad and I were very close. Dad was a rabid Yankees fan. He loved baseball and he used to drag me around to the games with him when it was just the two of us. It was his goal to see a game in every major league ballpark and he achieved that just before the leagues expanded. Then he threw up his hands and said, "Enough's enough!"

My dad was 5'11" tall with a slender build. Because he had skipped ahead in school, he was smaller than the

---

*An original account as told to Carol Jean Cook Coombs, February 2000.

other kids in his grade. Not especially athletic, he probably could identify with the guy who wasn't part of the reindeer games. I remember that he always loved the ugly duckling story and identified with the outcast who eventually found acceptance and admiration. My father, like Rudolph, came into his own at Christmas, with his Christmas story.

Certainly Rudolph changed our lives, but not immediately. My father remarried in 1941 and for a while each year there was one additional person in our little apartment (two sisters and a brother). Initially the Rudolph copyright belonged to Montgomery Ward, and millions of copies of the book were distributed free of charge. Then right after the War, Mr. Sewell Avery, a rather austere gentleman who presided over Montgomery Ward, generously gave the copyright to our father. That's when things changed. My father's youngest sister, Margaret, was married to composer Johnny Marks. In 1949, he put words and music to the Rudolph story and had the song published. Gene Autry recorded it. I heard that his wife liked it and persuaded him to put it on the backside of another record. It wasn't meant to be the main attraction.

Thanks to Rudolph, we were able to move to a home in Evanston, Illinois. I remember being very impressed with light switches that didn't make any noise when you turned them on or off. Two more sisters were born. Now there were six of us! About that time my father quit work to manage Rudolph-related enterprises. There were lots of products—odd things like musical toothbrush holders and wallpaper. Eventually things quieted down and he went back to work for Montgomery Wards. They had a motto that they would take anything back! We joked about that, how they took him back. He was always very proud of Wards.

Christmas was a shining time in the May household. All the usual rules were suspended. I used to leave snacks for Santa and I also had a correspondence of sorts with the Easter Bunny. Then one year I realized that Santa and the Easter bunny had the same handwriting. It was pretty disappointing until I realized all the work my parents went to. They even put up the Christmas tree after we were in bed to make it seem like Santa had done it.

We had a giant Rudolph, at least life-size, maybe larger, on the front lawn with a lighted nose and spangled reins. He leaned back like he was leaping up into the sky, not quite the diminutive deer you'd imagine.

Who could have known all those years ago when my dad tried out his Christmas story on me, his four-year-old daughter, that Rudolph would become part of our country's Christmas tradition!

Rudolph the Red-Nosed Reindeer

by

Robert L. May

'Twas the day before Christmas, and all through the hills
The reindeer were playing...enjoying the spills.
Of skating and coasting, and climbing the willows...
And hop-scotch and leap-frog (protected by pillows!).
While every so often they'd stop to call names
At one little deer not allowed in their games:
"Ha ha! Look at Rudolph! His nose is a sight!"
"It's red as a beet!" "Twice as big!" "Twice as bright!"
While Rudolph just cried.
What else could he do?
He knew that the things they were saying were true!
Where most reindeer's noses are brownish and tiny,
Poor Rudolph's was red, very large, and quite shiny.
In daylight it dazzled. (The picture shows that!)
At nighttime it glowed, like the eyes of a cat.
And putting dirt on it just made it look muddy.
(Oh boy, was he mad when they nicknamed him "Ruddy"!)
Although he was lonesome, he always was good...
Obeying his parents, as good reindeer should!
That's why, on this day, Rudolph almost felt playful:
He hoped that from Santa (soon driving his sleighful

Of presents and candy and dollies and toys
For good little animals, good girls and boys)
He'd get just as much...and this is what pleased him...
As the happier, handsomer reindeer who teased him.
So as night, and a fog, hid the world like a hood,
He went to bed hopeful, he knew he'd been good!
While way, way up North, on this same foggy night,
Old Santa was packing his sleigh for its flight.
"This fog," he complained, "will be hard to get through!"
He shook his round head. (And his tummy shook, too!)
"Without any stars or a moon as our compass,
This extra-dark night is quite likely to swamp us.
To keep from collisions, we'll have to fly slow.
To keep our direction, we'll have to fly low.
We'll steer by the street-lamps and houses tonight,
In order to finish before it gets light.
Just think how the boys' and girls' faith would be shaken,
If we didn't reach 'em before they awaken!"
"Come Dasher! Come Dancer! Come Prancer and Vixen!
Come Comet! Come Cupid! Come Donner and Blitzen!
Be quick with your suppers! Get hitched in a hurry!
You, too, will find fog a delay and a worry!"
And Santa was right. (As he usually is!)
The fog was as thick as a soda's white fizz.
Just not-getting-lost needed all Santa's skill...
With street-signs and numbers more difficult still.
He tangled in tree-tops again and again,
And barely missed hitting a four-motored plane.
He still made good speed, with much twisting and

turning
As long as the street-lamps and house-lights were burning.
At each house, first noting the people who live there,
He'd quickly pick out the right presents to give there.
By midnight, however, the last light had fled.
(For even big people have then gone to bed!)
Because it might wake them, a match was denied him.
(Oh my, how he wished for just one star to guide him!)
Through dark streets and houses old Santa did poorly.
He now picked the presents more slowly, less surely.
He really was worried! For what would he do,
If folks started waking before he was through?
The air was still foggy, the night dark and drear,
When Santa arrived at the home of the deer.
A ledge that he tripped on while seeking the chimney
Gave Santa a spill, and a painfully skinned-knee.
The room he came down in was blacker than ink,
He went for a chair, and then found it...a sink!
The first reindeer bedroom was so very black,
He tripped on the rug, and fell flat on his back.
So dark that he had to move close to the bed,
And squint very hard at the sleeping deer's head,
Before he could choose the right kind of a toy.
(A doll for a girl, or a train for a boy.)
But all this took time, and filled Santa with gloom,
While slowly he groped toward the next reindeer's room.
The door he'd just opened...when, to his surprise,
A dim but quite definite light met his eyes.
The lamp wasn't burning; the glow came, instead,
From something that lay at the head of the bed.

And there lay...but wait now! What would you suppose?
The glowing (you've guessed it) was RUDOLPH'S RED NOSE!"
So this room was easy!
This one little light
Let Santa pick quickly the gifts that were right.
How happy he was, till he went out the door...
The rest of the house was as black as before!
So black that it made every step a dark mystery.
And then...came the greatest idea in all history!
He went back to Rudolph and started to shake him
(Of course, very gently) in order to wake him.
And Rudolph could scarcely believe his own eyes!
You just can imagine his joy and surprise
At seeing who stood there, so real and so near,
While telling the tale we've already told here:
Poor Santa's sad story of dark and delay...
The fog and the blackness, and losing the way...
The horrible fear that some children might waken
Before his complete Christmas trip had been taken.
"And you," he told Rudolph, "may yet save the day!
Your wonderful forehead may yet pave the way
For a wonderful Christmas! It actually might!"
(Old Santa, you notice, was extra-polite
To Rudolph, regarding his "wonderful forehead."
To call it a "big, shiny nose" would sound horrid!)
"I need you," said Santa, "to help me tonight...
To lead all my deer on the rest of our flight."
And Rudolph broke out into such a big grin,
It almost connected his ears and his chin!
A note for his folks he dashed off in a hurry.
"I've gone to help Santa," he wrote. "Do not worry."
Said Santa: "My sleigh I'll bring down to the lawn.
You'd stick in the chimney." And *flash*...he was gone.

So Rudolph pranced out through the door, very gay,
And took his proud place at the head of the sleigh.
The rest of the night...well, what would you guess?
Old Santa's idea was a brilliant success.
And "brilliant" was almost no word for the way
That Rudolph directed the deer and the sleigh.
In spite of the fog, they flew quickly, and low,
And made such good use of the wonderful glow
From Rudolph's...er...forehead, at each intersection
That not even once did they lose their direction!
While as for the houses and streets with a sign on 'em,
They merely flew close, so that Rudolph could shine on 'em.
To tell who lived where, and just what to give whom,
They'd fly by each window and peek in the room.
Old Santa knew always which children were good,
And minded their parents, and ate as they should.
So Santa selected the gift that was right,
While Rudolph's..er..forehead gave just enough light.
It all went so fast, that before it was day,
The very last present was given away...
The very last stocking was filled to the top,
Just as the sun was preparing to pop.
This sun woke the reindeer in Rudolph's home town.
They found the short message that he'd written down...
Then gathered outside to await his return.
And were they excited, astonished, to learn
That Rudolph, the ugliest deer of them all,
(Rudolph the Red-nose...bashful and small...
The funny-faced fellow they always called names,
And practically never allowed in their games)
Was now to be envied by all, far and near.

For no greater honor can come to a deer
Than riding with Santa and guiding his sleigh!
The Number-One job, on the Number-One day!
The sleigh, and its reindeer, soon came into view.
And Rudolph still led them, as downward they flew.
Oh boy, was he proud, as they came to a landing
Right where his handsomer playmates were standing!
These bad deer who used to do nothing but tease him
Would now have done anything...only to please him!
They felt even sorrier they had been bad
When Santa said: "Rudolph, I never have had
A deer quite so brave or so brilliant as you
At fighting black fog, and at steering me through.
By YOU last night's journey was actually bossed.
Without you, I'm certain we'd all have been lost!
I hope you'll continue to keep us from grief,
On future dark trips, as COMMANDER-IN-CHIEF!"
While Rudolph just blushed, from his head to his toes,
Until his whole fur was as red as his nose!
The crowd first applauded, then started to screech:
"Hurray for our Rudolph!" and "We want a speech!"
But Rudolph was bashful, despite being a hero!
And tired! (His sleep on the trip totaled zero.)
So that's why his speech was quite short, and not bright:
"Merry Christmas to all, and to all a good night"...
and THAT'S WHY...
......whenever it's foggy and gray,
It's Rudolph the Red-nose who guides Santa's sleigh.
Be listening, this Christmas! (But don't make a peep...
'Cause that late at night, children should be asleep!)

The very first sound that you'll hear on the roof
(Provided there's fog) will be Rudolph's small hoof.
And soon after that (if you're still as a mouse)
You may hear a "swish" as he flies 'round the house,
And gives enough light to give Santa a view
Of you and your room. And when they're all through,
You may hear them call, as they drive out of sight:
"MERRY CHRISTMAS TO ALL, AND TO ALL A
GOOD NIGHT!"

VI

We Three Kings

Across the centuries and over the seas, the Christmas story has thrived and changed countless lives for the better. Since that first Christmas, many have tried to capture its spirit in other words, other stories.

These last three stories are the tales of three kings: A prose version of an old English carol about Christ-like love and service; the story of a wise man who, although he never found the child in the manger, served the Savior throughout his life; and a story about the greatest King of all, and his gift to a little shepherd boy.

I had always wanted a prose version of the traditional carol, "Good King Wenceslas," and was pleased when I found "The Good King" by well-known children's author Natalie Babbitt.

The original version of "The Other Wiseman" is too long to tell easily, so I was delighted to find this adaptation by Sterling W. Sill, an excellent storyteller who had a Sunday evening radio show. He shortened this story to "tellable" form for his program, and fortunately it was printed.

"The Anniversary" is our family's favorite. I've often been invited to tell a story at Christmas gatherings and when I use this story, someone usually asks for a copy. I first read it from a library book, *The Lights of Christmas,* while the rest of the family napped one Christmas afternoon thirty years ago.

May you have a Merry Christmas, filled with the star's true light.

The Good King

by

Natalie Babbitt

PART ONE: The King and the Page

The King stood at the window, sipping at a mug of hot mulled wine and looking out. "It's a rude night," he said to no one in particular as the wind, leaning hard against the easement, moaned and tossed up spirals of dry white snowflakes. Then the King, looking down, noticed a stooping figure moving slowly across the field below, its shadow pale blue under the moon.

"Bless my soul!" said the King, "Who can that be?" He turned and beckoned to a young page who was warming himself before the blaze in a great stone fireplace across the room. "Here, lad, come and tell me if you know who that is down there."

The page came over to the window and peered out. "It looks like the old peasant who lives near the forest, sire," he said. "Three miles or so from here."

"Whatever is he doing down there?" asked the King, pressing his face against the glass to see better.

"I think he's picking up firewood, sire," said the page.

The King rubbed a little hole in the circle of frost his breath had made on the window and squinted through it. "There he goes," he said. "He's got a good load of twigs and he's going away, poor fellow." He scratched at his

---

"The Good King" by Natalie Babbitt. Published in *Redbook* magazine December 1971. Reprinted by permission of the author.

beard for a moment and then his face lighted up. "Tell you what, lad. Bring me a bottle of wine, a side of venison and some good pine logs, and we'll take them to him, you and I."

"Now?" said the page. "Through the snow? At night?"

"Certainly!" said the king. "Do you know how to find his cottage?"

"I think so," said the page doubtfully, "but it's very dark out."

"We'll find it," said the King. "Run and get everything together, and don't forget a good warm cloak."

PART TWO: The Peasants

"It's a rude night," said the old man as he came stamping and blowing through the door of the cottage. "Cold and dark as an overlord's heart!" He put down his load of twigs beside the hearth and held out his hands to the fire.

"Never mind," said his old woman, beaming at him. "You're home at last. And look here in the pot—we'll be having a fine supper for Saint Stephen's Day. I sold two yards of cloth in the village today, so there's a carrot and a chunk of onion to dress up your rabbit, and a bowl of hot milk for each of us, and a bit of good bread. Not a morsel to spare, but enough is as good as a feast, they say."

"So they do," said the old man. He pulled up a stool before the fire and watched as the old woman stirred the pot. "I looked up at the castle and saw the King standing in the window," he told her.

"Did you, now?" she said. "Well, he's a good man, the King is. But no better a man than you, at that. And he can have his castle. We've enough, you and I. A good supper, a warm bed and firewood to last the night. Better off than some, no doubt."

"Better off than many," said the old man. "Though I'm bound to say I've no heart for sharing tonight, seeing there's just enough for two."

"Enough is as good as a feast," the old woman said.

"So they say." He nodded. "So they say."

PART THREE: The King and the Page

The wind, growing wilder every moment, scooped up great clouds of snow and whirled them high into the bitter darkness. "Hey there, lad!" the King boomed cheerfully through his layers of mufflers. "Are we nearly there?"

The page, weighted down with a sturdy pine log under each arm and a bottle of wine slung in a sack over his shoulder, dragged to a halt in snow to his knees and tried to see through the tears that the wind slapped streaming from his eyes. "I think I'm lost!" he called back through the blast. "It's so dark and the wind blows so, I can't see anything!"

"Here!" called the King. "Let me go first. I'm bigger. You can walk in my footsteps." He waded up alongside the page and peered through the darkness.

"But you don't know how to find the cottage, sire," the page protested. "If you go first, we'll be lost for sure. And I'm nearly done in as it is."

"We'll find it," the King assured him. "Leave those logs behind. I've got these two"—he adjusted the pair of logs under his own arms and shifted the weight of the side of roasted venison, which was slowly stiffening in its sling across his chest—"and two is better than none. We'll find it, lad. Come along."

The King pushed ahead and the page, dropping his logs into the snow, struggled after him. The bottle of wine banged against his back, the wind drove home under his cloak and his legs felt numb. The going was easier in the King's wake, but the page was slender and far from strong. At last he stopped and sat down in the snow. "I'm sorry, sire," he called, "but I can't go another step."

The King turned. "No—no, lad! Don't sit down. It can't be much farther."

"I think we've been going in circles," said the page wearily. "I'm so tired—I want to rest."

The King dropped his own two logs into the snow, lifted the sling of venison off over his head and let that fall as well. "Here, lad," he said gently. "I'd better carry you." And he took the boy up in his arms and pushed forward.

PART FOUR: All Together

"Now!" said the old woman. "It's ready. Come and sit." She spooned out the steaming stew onto two plates, scraping the sides of the pot with great care to collect every drop. The old man sat down gratefully at the table and was just lifting his bowl of milk to his lips when a banging came at the door.

"Bless my soul!" said the old woman. "Who can that be?"

They threw open the door and the King staggered in, frosted from head to toe, with the young page in his arms.

"Dear heaven!" cried the old man, dropping to his knees. "It's the King!"

"Alas, my dear fellow!" gasped the King. "My poor page is near frozen to death. We were coming to you with gifts for Saint Stephen's Day, but we lost our way in the snow and had to leave the gifts behind."

"It's a rude night, sire, for sure," said the old woman, latching the door. "Lay the lad down on the bed and I'll give him this hot milk. He's gone all blue with cold."

One bowl of milk and then the other, and when the page began to revive a little, they wrapped him in a blanket and the King came away from the bed to stand before the fire, warming his hands while the melting snow ran from his cloak into little pools at his feet. The old woman took up her plate of stew and held it out shyly to him. “Here, sire—you need a bit of warming up yourself.”

“But see here, my dear woman, this is your supper!” the King protested.

“Never you mind,” said the old woman to ease his distress. “There’s enough for us all right here, and enough is as good as a feast.”

PART FIVE: The Peasants

“To think,” said the old man, “to think that the King himself slept in our bed last night!”

“And ate with us too,” said the old woman. “A thing never to be forgotten.”

“He’s a good man, the King is, coming out into the snow like that just to bring gifts to the likes of us,” the old man said.

“Yes, he’s a good man,” the old woman answered. “But no better a man than you, at that. I’ve made you a good soup with the bones of the rabbit, and there was a bit of onion still. Come and sit.”

And they ate their soup and thought about the night before and marveled.

The Other Wiseman

by

Henry Van Dyke

adapted by Sterling W. Sill

Each year at Christmas time we delight to follow the wise men as they come out of the East and make their way to Bethlehem where they worship the newborn King and lay their treasures at His feet.

Henry Van Dyke has told us about another wise man who might have followed the star, not only to Bethlehem but throughout his life: and yet he never found the King. His name was Artaban. He was a kind of unknown soldier who did not quite make the headlines. He was also one of the Magi and lived in Persia. He was a man of great wealth, great learning, and great faith. With his learned companions, he had searched the scriptures as to the time that the Saviour should be born. They knew that a new star would appear, and it was agreed between them that Artaban would watch from Persia and that the others would observe the sky from Babylon.

On the night that the sign was to be given, Artaban spoke to nine of his Magi friends in his home. He said to them, "My three brethren are watching at the ancient temple of the Seven Spheres, at Borsippa, in Babylon; and I am watching here. If the star appears, they will wait for me ten days; then we will all set out together for Jerusalem. I believe the sign will come tonight. I have

---

made ready for the journey by selling all of my possessions and have bought these three jewels—a sapphire, a ruby, and a pearl. I intend to present them as my tribute to the king." He said, "I invite you to make this pilgrimage with us that we may worship the newborn king together."

While he spoke, he thrust his hand into the inmost fold of his girdle and drew out three great gems—one blue as a fragment of the night sky, one redder than a ray of the sunrise, and one as pure as the peak of a snow mountain at twilight. He would give them all to the king. Then one of Artaban's friends said, "Artaban, this is a vain dream. No king will ever rise from the broken race of Israel. He who looks for him is a chaser of shadows." Then he bid Artaban farewell and left his dwelling.

Each in turn offered his own particular excuse, and finally only his oldest and truest friend remained. He said, "Artaban, I am too old for this quest, but my heart goes with thee." Then with a hand on Artaban's shoulder, he said, "Those who would see wonderful things must often be willing to travel alone."

Left to himself, Artaban put his jewels back into his girdle. Then he parted the curtains and went out onto the roof to again take up his vigil to watch the night sky.

As Jupiter and Saturn rolled together like drops of lambent flame about to blend into one, an azure spark was born out of the darkness beneath them. The spark grew, rounding itself with purple splendor into a crimson sphere.

Artaban bowed his head. "It is the sign," he said. "The king is coming, and I will go to meet him."

All night long Vasda, the swiftest of Artaban's horses, had been waiting saddled and bridled in her stall, pawing the ground impatiently and shaking her bit as if she shared the eagerness of her master.

As Artaban placed himself upon her back, he said, "God bless us both, and keep our feet from falling and our souls from death."

Under his encouragement, each day his faithful horse measured off the allotted proportion of the distance; and, at nightfall of the tenth day, they approached the outskirts of Babylon. In a little island of desert palm trees, Vasda scented difficulty and slackened her pace. Then she gave a quick breath of anxiety and stood stock-still, quivering in every muscle.

Artaban dismounted. The dim starlight revealed the form of a man lying in the roadway. His humble dress and haggard face showed him to be one of the poor Hebrew exiles who still dwelt in Babylon. His pallid skin bore the mark of the deadly fever that ravished the marshlands of Babylon at this season of the year. The chill of death was in his lean hand. As Artaban turned to go, a sigh came from the sick man's lips; and the brown, bony fingers closed convulsively upon the Magian's robe.

Artaban felt sorry that he could not stay to minister to this dying stranger, but this was the hour toward which his entire life had been directed. He could not forfeit the reward of his years of study and faith to do a single deed of human mercy. But then, how could he leave his fellow man alone to die?

"God of truth and mercy," prayed Artaban, "direct me in the holy path of wisdom which only thou knowest." Then he knew that he could not go on. The Magians were physicians as well as astronomers. He took off his robe and began his work of healing. Several hours later the patient regained consciousness.

Then Artaban gave him all he had left of bread and wine. He left a potion of healing herbs and instructions for his care.

Though Artaban rode with the greatest haste the

rest of the way, it was after dawn when he arrived at the designated meeting place. His friends were nowhere to be seen. Finally his eyes caught a piece of parchment arranged to attract his attention. He caught it up and read. It said, "We have waited till past the midnight and can delay no longer. We go to find the King. Follow us across the desert."

Artaban sat down upon the ground in despair and covered his face with his hands. "How can I cross the desert," said he, "with no food and with a spent horse? I must return to Babylon, sell my sapphire, and buy a train of camels and provisions for the journey. I may never overtake my friends. Only God the merciful knows whether or not I shall lose my purpose because I tarried to show mercy."

Several days later when Artaban's train arrived at Bethlehem, the streets were deserted. It was rumored that Herod was sending soldiers, presumably to enforce some new tax; and the men had taken their flocks and herds back into the hills beyond his reach.

The door of one dwelling was open, and Artaban could hear a mother singing a lullaby to her child. He entered and introduced himself. The woman told him that it was now the third day since the three wise men had appeared in Bethlehem. They had found Joseph and Mary and the young child, and they had laid their gifts at his feet. Then they disappeared as mysteriously as they had come. Joseph had taken his wife and babe that same night and had secretly fled into Egypt.

As Artaban listened, the baby reached up its dimpled hand and touched his cheek and smiled. His heart warmed at the touch. Then suddenly outside there arose a wild confusion of sounds. Women were shrieking. Then a desperate cry said, "The soldiers of Herod are killing the children!"

Artaban went to the doorway. A band of soldiers came hurrying down the street with dripping swords and bloody hands. The captain approached the door to thrust Artaban aside, but Artaban did not stir. His face was as calm as though he were still watching the stars. Finally his outstretched hand revealed the giant ruby. He said, "I am waiting to give this jewel to the prudent captain who will go on his way and leave this house alone."

The captain, amazed at the splendor of the gem, took it and said to his men, "March on, there are no children here."

Then Artaban prayed, "Oh God, forgive me my sin. I have spent for man that which was meant for God. Shall I ever be worthy to see the face of the King?"

But the voice of the woman weeping for joy in the shadows behind him said softly, "Because thou hast saved the life of my little one, may the Lord bless thee and keep thee; the Lord maketh His face to shine upon thee and be gracious unto thee; the Lord lift up His countenance upon thee and give thee peace."

Then Artaban, still following the King, went on into Egypt, seeking for traces of the little family that had fled before him from Bethlehem.

For many years Artaban continued in his search. He was seen at the pyramids. He was seen in an obscure house in Alexandria, taking counsel from a Hebrew rabbi who told him to seek the king not among the rich but among the poor. He passed through countries where famine lay heavy upon the land and the poor cried for bread. He made his dwelling in plague-stricken cities where the sick languished in the bitter companionship of helpless misery. He visited the oppressed and the afflicted in the gloom of subterranean prisons. He searched the crowded wretchedness of slavemarkets. Though he found no one to worship, he found many to serve. As the years passed, he fed the hungry, clothed the naked, healed the sick, and comforted the captive.

In time, Artaban stood alone at sunrise, waiting at the gate of a Roman prison. He had taken from its secret resting place in his bosom the last of his jewels that he had saved for the King. Shifting gleams of azure and rose trembled upon its surface. It seemed to have absorbed some of the colors of the lost sapphire and ruby; just as a noble life draws into itself its profound purpose so that all that has helped it is transfused into its very essence, so the pearl had become more precious because it had long been carried close to the warmth of a beating human heart.

Thirty-three years had passed away since Artaban began his search and he was still a pilgrim. His hair was now white as snow. He knew his life's end was near, but he was still desperate with hopes that he would yet find the King. For this purpose he had come for the last time to Jerusalem.

It was the season of the Passover, and the city was thronged with strangers. There was a singular agitation visible in the multitude. A secret human tide was sweeping them toward the Damascus gate.

Artaban inquired where they were going. One answered, "We are going to the execution on Golgotha, outside the city walls. Two robbers are to be crucified, and with them a man called Jesus of Nazareth, a man who has done many wonderful works among the people. But the priests and elders have said that He must die, because He claims to be the Son of God. Pilate sent Him to the cross, because He said that He was the King of the Jews."

How strangely these familiar words fell upon the tired heart of Artaban. They had led him for a lifetime over land and sea. And now they came to him darkly and mysteriously like a message of despair. The King had been denied and cast out. He was now about to perish. Perhaps

He was already dying. Could He be the same for whom the star had appeared thirty-three long years ago?

Artaban's heart beat loudly within him. He thought, "The ways of God are stranger than the thoughts of men, and it may be that I shall yet find the King and be able to ransom Him from death by giving my treasure to His enemies."

But as Artaban started toward Calvary, he saw a troop of Macedonian soldiers coming down the street, dragging a sobbing young woman with torn dress and disheveled hair. As Artaban paused, she broke away from her tormentors and threw herself at his feet, clasping her arms around his knees.

"Have pity on me," she cried, "and save me, for the sake of the God of purity. My father was also of the Magi, but he is dead; and I am to be sold as a slave to pay his debts."

Artaban trembled as he again felt the old conflict arising in his soul. It was the same that he had experienced in the palm grove of Babylon and in the cottage at Bethlehem. Twice the gift which he had consecrated to the King had been drawn from his hand to the service of humanity. Would he now fail again? One thing was clear—he must rescue this helpless child from evil.

He took the pearl from his bosom. Never had it seemed so luminous, so radiant, so full of tender, living luster. He laid it in the hand of the slave and said, "Daughter, this is thy ransom. It is the last of my treasures which I had hoped to keep for the King."

While he yet spoke, the darkness of the sky thickened and the shuddering tremors of an earthquake ran through the ground.

The houses rocked. The soldiers fled in terror. Artaban sank beside a wall. What had he to fear? What had he to hope for? He had given away the last remnant of his tribute to the King. The quest was over, and he had failed. What else mattered? As one lingering pulsation of the earthquake quivered beneath him, a heavy tile, shaken from a roof, fell and struck him on the temple. He lay breathless and pale. The rescued girl leaned over him, fearing that he was dead. Then there came a still, small voice through the twilight. It was like distant music. The notes were clear, but the girl could not understand the words.

Then the lips of Artaban began to move, as if in answer; and she heard him say, "Not so, my Lord: For when saw I thee an hungered and fed thee? Or thirsty, and gave thee drink? When saw I thee a stranger, and took thee in? Or naked, and clothed thee? When saw I thee sick or in prison and came unto thee? Thirty-three years have I looked for thee; but I have never seen they face nor ministered unto thee, my King."

He ceased, and the sweet voice came again. And again the maid heard it, very faintly and far away. But now she understood the words which said, "Verily, I say unto thee, that inasmuch as thou hast done it unto one of the least of these my brethren, thou hast done it unto me."

A calm radiance of wonder and joy lighted the face of Artaban as one long, last breath exhaled gently from his lips. His journey was ended. His treasures were accepted. The "Other Wise Man" had found the King.

The Anniversary

by

Margaret Sangster

The boy sat quite alone on the hilltop, his shepherd's crook across his knees, his small square lunch basket beside him. He made an odd, distorted shadow in the white light of the moon, for even the fringed shawl that his mother had woven of lamb's wool could not hide the ugly hump that lay—a burden much too heavy for so young a lad to bear—between his shoulders.

Far below him, dotting the hillside with other irregular shadows, were the sheep. The majority of them slept, but a few wandered aimlessly up and down the slope. The boy, however, was not watching the flock. His head was thrown back, and his wide eyes were fixed on the sky.

"Perhaps it will happen again," he was thinking, "perhaps—though a third of a century has gone by. Perhaps I shall see the great star and hear the angel voices as my father did!"

The moon, riding high in the heavens, went under a blanket of clouds. For a moment the world was dark. The boy sighed and lowered his eyes.

"It is an omen," he breathed, "an omen! Though it is the time of anniversary, there will be no star this night. Neither will the angels sing...."

The time of anniversary. How often the boy had listened to the story of the miracle that had taken place so long ago! The boy's father had been a lad himself then—

---

he had been the youngest of the shepherds on that glorious occasion when an angel anthem sounded across the world and a star shone above the tranquil town of Bethlehem. The boy's father had followed the star; with the other shepherds he had come to the stable of the inn. Crowding through the narrow doorway, he had seen a woman with a baby in her arms.

"But—" the boy's father had told the story so many times that his family and the neighbors knew it word for word— "she was no ordinary woman! There was something in her face that made one think of a lighted candle. And there was a tenderness in her smile that the very cattle felt, for they drew close to her and seemed to kneel. It was not her beauty, although beauty she did possess! It was a shine from within—"

"And the baby—" the boy always prompted his father here—"what of the baby?"

The father's hand touched his small son's shoulder at this point—touched it, and drew away.

"The baby," he said, and his voice grew hushed, "was as unlike other infants as his mother was different from other women. Scarce an hour old when first I glimpsed him, there was a sense of wisdom—no, do not laugh—on his brow, and his tiny up-curled hands seemed—indeed, I do mean it!—to hold power. I found myself kneeling, as the cattle knelt, and there was the damp of tears upon my face, and—though I was a lad tall for my age—I was not ashamed."

Alone on the hillside, the boy could almost hear the sound of his father's voice in the stillness. His father's voice telling the story of the marvelous infant and of the Wise Men who had come to the stable—following, also, in the path of the star. They had come bearing gifts, the fame of which traveled through all the land. Often the boy had heard of the gold and frankincense and myrrh; often he had shivered at the tale of the great cruel king who had ordered death to all male infants. Often he had thrilled to the saga of a worried mother—and her sober husband—who had stolen away into the land of Egypt with her child.

"Many of us thought," the boy's father finished, "that the child had been captured and slain by Herod. Until a decade passed and we heard rumors of a youth who bore his name, and who lectured in a temple at Jerusalem to a group of learned doctors. A few years ago we heard that this same youth, grown older, had organized a band of men, that with them he was journeying from place to place, preaching and teaching and aiding the needy. And—" here the boy's father had a habit of lowering his voice and glancing furtively around the room— "there are some who say that he has become a Messiah, and that he does more than champion the cause of the common people. There are some who say that he performs wonderful deeds, healing the halt and the blind and the lepers—even raising the dead."

Once, at this point, the boy interrupted. "I would that I might meet him," he had said with ill-masked eagerness. "I would that he might take the hump from my back and make me strong and straight like other children."

It was growing cold on the hillside. The child drew the shawl closer about his tired body and wished that he were not a shepherd. Shepherds led a lonely life—they did not fit into the bright places of the world. Rooms gaily lighted at eventide were for the men and boys who worked hard by day and earned their moments of ease; they were not for shepherds. But what else could a crippled lad do to justify his existence—what else than tend sheep? A crippled lad who could not undertake physical labor and who had no talents.

Yawning wearily, the boy glanced at the sky. From the position of the moon he judged it to be middle night—it was still a long while before sunrise; still hours before someone would come to take his place and he could limp home. And yet middle night had its compensations! For at that time he could break his fast and partake of the lunch that his mother had packed so neatly into a basket.

As he reached for the basket, opening it slowly, the boy was wondering what had been prepared for his refreshment. He found, to his satisfaction, that there was a flask of goat's milk, and nearly a loaf of crusty dark bread, and some yellow cheese; and there were dried figs, sugary with their own sweetness. And, wrapped separately, he came upon a real treat. A cake made of eggs and sifted flour, with citron in it, and raisins!

He had expected the bread and the cheese and the milk. Even the figs he had expected. But the cake was a surprise, the sort of surprise that happened seldom. His eyes gleamed as he surveyed it, and some of the sadness went out of them. Carefully he set the basket down and spread on the ground beside him the swath of linen in which his mother had folded the lunch. Carefully he laid out the flask of milk, the bread, the cheese—but not the cake, which he left tucked away in the depths of the basket. He left it there so that he might not be tempted to eat it first!

"It is good to be hungry," he said aloud. "Yes—and to have food!"

From somewhere just behind him a voice spoke. It was not a loud voice, and yet the music of it seemed to carry beyond the hillside.

"Indeed, yes!" said the voice. "It is good to be hungry. And to have food, and to—"

Startled, for he had thought he was quite alone with his thoughts and the drowsing sheep, the boy glanced back across his crooked shoulder. He saw a man standing upon the brow of the hill, silhouetted against the night sky. Ordinarily he would have known fear, for there were cruel robbers abroad often at middle night. But somehow the sight of this man, who was tall and muscular, failed to frighten him. He did not know why he instinctively completed the man's unfinished sentence.

"And to share it!" he murmured, as if in a dream. "You are a stranger, sir?"

The man came closer to the child and stood looking down upon him. "No, not a stranger," he said slowly, "never a stranger. As it happens, my journey started not far from this very place—started years before you, my lad, saw the light. I am by way of completing a circle."

Although he couldn't imagine what the man meant, the boy made swift response.

"I was about to eat my lunch," he said, indicating the square of linen on which he had arranged the contents of his basket. "One grows ravenous on the hillside. I am a shepherd, sir. I tend my father's flock, and each night my mother packs for me a simple repast. Will you be seated—you who have journeyed so long—and break bread with me? Perhaps—" he hesitated shyly— "you will talk with me as we eat? It grows lonely on the dark hillside—I pine at times for companionship."

The man continued to peer down from his impressive height. His eyes held a warm glow—it was as if a candle burned somewhere behind them, the boy thought, and remembered words that his father had spoken when he described a woman in a stable. He felt so comforted by the man's glance that he smiled up into the kindly face, and the man spoke again.

"It is a strange coincidence," he said, "the fact that you are a shepherd, for I also tend my father's flock! And I also—" his smile was luminous— "have often grown lonely waiting for the gates of dawn to open. Are you sure—" he seated himself upon the ground— "that you have enough for two? I should not like to deprive you of anything."

Gazing, fascinated, into the man's face, the boy replied:

"But, yes! I have a large flask of goat's milk, and some yellow cheese, and nearly a loaf of bread, and ten figs. And..." for a second he hesitated, "that's a great plenty," he finished lamely. He did not mention the cake, still wrapped in the basket. For a cake—a cake made of sifted flour and eggs and citron and raisins—was a rare delicacy. And it was not a very big cake.

The man bent forward to retie the thong of a sandal. The boy saw that the sandal was covered with dust. He tried to keep his eyes from glancing toward his lunch basket as he tore the crusty dark bread into fragments.

"Perhaps your feet are aching," he ventured as he placed the fragments in the center of the linen cloth. "This hill is hard to climb. I am close to being spent when I reach the summit of it, but I must sit high so that I can watch all the sheep."

The man said slowly: "I have climbed steeper hills than this one, my lad, and know that there are steeper hills to be. My feet do not ache. How long— "abruptly he changed the subject— "have you been crippled?"

Had it come from an ordinary person, the boy would have resented such a display of curiosity. From this man the question seemed a natural one, to be answered naturally.

"Why," he said, "I have never been without a hump between my shoulders. I hate it, but—" he was quoting his mother— "what must be, must be! Still—" his childish face was a trifle unchildish— "it is hard to go through life looking like one of the camels that the Wise Men rode when they came from the east—"

The man interrupted. "What, lad," he queried, "do you know of the Wise Men from the east? How does it happen that you should mention them to me on this night? It is—" he bit into a piece of the crusty dark bread—"very curious!"

Laughing softly, the little boy answered. "I suppose the Wise Men are in my mind," he said, "Because this is the time of anniversary, and I have been thinking of the baby that was born in a stable. I was hoping—before you arrived—that once again the great star might shine and that the angels might sing. I have, in fact, been watching the sky rather than the sheep."

The man asked another swift question. "What," he queried, "do you know about these holy things—about the star—the song? You are so very young!"

The boy explained. "All Bethlehem," he said, "heard about the star, and about the infant who lay in the manger because there was no room at the inn. I know, perhaps, more than the others, for my father—a child then himself—was one of the shepherds who saw the light from the heavens and heard the angel music. Will you—" the boy had taken the flask of goat's milk into his hands—"will you share with me this cup, sir? For perhaps you thirst?"

The man took the flask from the fragile hands. His fingers were powerful and sinewy, but as gentle as a woman's. He said,

"I will share the cup with you, my lad, for I do thirst."

As he watched the man drinking deeply, the boy thought, "It must be tiring to tramp from place to place."

He said on impulse, as the stranger set down the flask, "Will you tell me, sir, of some of the towns in which you have stayed?"

The man answered: “One town is very like another, my lad, with poverty and pain rubbing elbows against wealth, with greed taking toll, all too often, of humanity. With health on one side and illness on the other. With so few gracious deeds that one can do to help the sore distressed—” he turned his face away— “and a lifetime in which to do them so desperately short!”

In a low tone the boy said: “Sometimes, when I was a tot, I hoped that my life might be short, but already I am ten years old. How old, sir, are you? I feel older than my years...”

The man’s voice was muted as he replied, “I am more than three times your age, lad, but I, too, feel older than my years.”

“You shouldn’t, because you’re so strong,” the boy exclaimed. “When is your time of birth, sir? I was born when it was spring.”

The man smiled his beautiful, luminous smile. “It’s odd that you should ask, dear lad,” he murmured, “for this is my day of birth. You, quite unknowing, are giving me an anniversary feast and never has a feast been more welcome. I was weary and forlorn when I came upon you.”

Weary and forlorn! As he stared at the man, the little boy queried:

“Haven’t you any people of your own? People with whom you can make merry on your day of birth? When my birthday arrives, Mother prepares a real feast for me, and gives me gifts. This shawl I wear she wove for my last birthday. The year before she pressed a sheaf of bright flowers into wax. Once, when I was smaller, she made wondrous sweetmeats of honey and grain.”

The man reached over and rested his hand on the little boy’s knee. “I fear,” he said, “that I have grown too old and large for birthday gifts. Furthermore, my loved ones are not near enough just now to make merry with me. But maybe, who knows, there will be a gift for me at my journey's end."

The boy's knee felt all atingle under the pressure of the friendly hand. He asked, "When, sir, will you come to your journey's end?"

The man did not meet the child's gaze. He replied, "Perhaps very soon!"

The boy was worried. He said: "You don't look happy about it. Don't you want to come to the end of your travels? Don't you want to reach them and see what gift they have in store for you?"

The man hesitated ever so slightly. "Yes," he said at last, "I want to reach—home. But the gift—it may be too beautiful to bear. Or too heavy for me to carry. I suppose—" his face looked drawn in the white moonlight— "I should be getting on. You have made this birthday very sweet, my lad!"

Peeping down at the white cloth with its remnants of bread and cheese, the boy thought: "There seems to be as much food as ever! He couldn't have liked it." Suddenly he was swept by a burning sense of shame. He spoke impetuously, one word tumbling over the other.

"You did not enjoy your food," he said, "and you have no true birthday feast. That—though you have no way of guessing—is because I have been selfish and mean! I," he gulped out his confession, "have a cake in my basket—a cake that I was saving to eat alone after you left me. It is a cake of sifted flour and eggs and citron and raisins, *and I love cake.* But now," the boy's voice quavered, "I would not enjoy it if I ate it in a solitary fashion; it would choke me! Sir, I desire to give the cake to you as my gift. Perhaps you will munch it later, when the chill of early morn has set in and you are on the road."

The man did not speak, but his eyes were like stars—instead of candles—as he watched his small host lift the cake from the basket and display its rich goodness. It was only when the boy extended it toward him that he broke into speech.

"Ah, my lad," he said, "you have sustained me with your bread, and we have drunk deep of the same cup. So now we will share this cake, which shall be, through your bounty, my birthday cake. We will apportion it evenly and deftly, and we will eat of it together—you and I. And then you shall wait for the dawn, and I will be on my way. But as I walk along the road I shall see a little lad's face, and shall hear a little lad's voice, and shall remember a little lad's generosity."

Gravely—as if he were handling something infinitely precious—the man took the rich cake into his fingers. Carefully, he divided it so that the two sections were equal. He said, "Bless unto us this food, my Father," and the boy was startled, because there was no one else upon the hillside. Then he said,

"This is the cake of life, lad. Enjoy it to the last crumb!"

So he and the boy ate the cake together, and the boy thought that he had never tasted such fare. It was as if the cake's richness were verily the richness of life! As he licked the last crumbs from his fingers, he felt that he was gathering force and vigor and purpose. In his mind's eye, for no reason at all, he saw a picture of himself—robust and handsome and brave—striding down the road with his weakness cast from him and his chin high.

"It's like a vision!" he said, but when the man queried,

"What do you mean, lad?" he hung his head and was unable to answer.

Indeed, he was silent so long that the man's hand came to rest lightly upon his shoulder—lightly, but, oh, so firmly! There was something in the touch that made tears hang on the boy's lashes, that wrung from him quick words.

"Oh," he cried, "do not leave me, sir! We could be such friends, you and I. Come with me to my home and dwell with my family. My mother will bake many cakes for you, and my father will share with you of his plenty. And I—you may have my bed, and my waxed flowers, and even this fringed shawl that I wear. Do not journey on, sir! Stay with me, here in Bethlehem."

The man spoke. His voice was like a great bell tolling over hill and valley. "I must go on," he said. "I must be about my father's business—I must travel toward my destiny. But I shall never leave you, my lad, for all that. Lo, I am with you always—even unto the end of the world!"

Bowing his head in his hands, covering his misted eyes, the boy was aware of the man's firm fingers traveling up from his shoulder until they touched his hair. But now he couldn't speak, for a pulse drummed in his throat, and a strange rhythm was hammering in his ears. When he raised his head, finally, the man was gone, and the hillside was empty—save for the shadows that were the sheep.

The boy sobbed once, and sharply, with a sense of loss. He struggled to his feet. Only he didn't have to struggle, really, for there was a curious lightness about his body, and a feeling of freshness and peace—a peace that transcended the pain of parting. But it was not until he drew the fringed lamb's wool shawl tighter across his back that he realized how straight he was standing—and how straight he would always stand.

Acknowledgments

Many thanks to the following authors and publishers for permission to reprint these stories.

I. A Child's Gift

"Trouble at the Inn" by Dina Donahue. Reprinted with permission from *Guideposts* magazine, copyright (c) 1965 by Guideposts, Carmel, New York 10512.

"A Christmas Gift I'll Never Forget" by L.D. Hummel. First published in *Parents* magazine, copyright (c) 1992 Gruner + Jahr USA Publishing. Reprinted from *Parents* magazine by permission. Reprinted with permission from the December 1994 *Reader's Digest.*

"Christmas Day in the Morning" by Pearl Buck. Reprinted by permission of Harold Ober Associates Incorporated. Copyright (c) 1955 by Pearl S. Buck. Copyright renewed 1983.

"Rich in Christmas Spirit" by Angela Gionfriddo. First published in *Woman's Day*, December 21, 1991.

"Carla's Gift" by Torey Hayden. Copyright (c) 1994 by Torey Hayden. First appeared in *Family Circle Magazine.* Printed by permission of Curtis Brown, Ltd.

II. I Was a Stranger

"How Santa Spread Cheer Without Eight Tiny Reindeer" by Rip Rense. Published December 22, 1991. Copyright 1991, *Los Angeles Times*. Reprinted by permission.

"Then We Found the Rocking Horse" by Derek Dixon, (c) Church of Jesus Christ of Latter-day Saints. First published in *The Ensign,* December 1973. Used by permission.

"Used Car Dealer Plays Santa" by *Ventura County Star Free Press,* December 1981. Copyright *Ventura County Star*. Reprinted by permission.

"Two Festivals of Light" from *Seven Stories of Christmas Love,* by Leo Buscaglia. Copyright 1987. Published by Slack, Inc. Used by permission.

III. Morning of Miracles

"The Gold and Ivory Tablecloth" by Howard C. Shade. Reprinted with permission from the December 1954 *Reader's Digest*. Copyright (c) 1954 by The Reader's Digest Assn., Inc.

"A Christmas Full of Determination" by Emil Busch, published in the *Thousand Oaks Chronicle*. Copyright, *Ventura County Star*. Reprinted by permission.

"My Christmas Miracle" by Taylor Caldwell. Copyright (c) 1961 by Taylor Caldwell. Reprinted by permission of William Morris Agency, Inc. on behalf of the author.

"An Exchange of Gifts" by Diane Rayner. Reprinted with permission from *Guideposts* magazine. Copyright (c) 1983 by Guideposts, Carmel, NY 10512.

IV. And On Earth Peace

"Christmas Eve in the Stable" by David Niven. Published in *Christmas with Ed Sullivan*, written and compiled by Ed Sullivan, published in 1959 by The McGraw-Hill Companies. Reprinted by permission of The McGraw-Hill Company.

"A Christmas Ballad for the Captain" by William J. Lederer from *A Happy Book of Christmas Stories*. Reprinted with permission from the author.

"Christmas Day, Italy, 1943" by Walter Stevenson, (c) Church of Jesus Christ of Latter-day Saints. First published in *The Ensign*, December 1973. Used by permission.

"The Creche" by Glenn Kittler originally appeared in *Daily Guideposts*, 1985. Reprinted with permission from *Daily Guideposts*, 1985. Copyright (c) 1984 by Guideposts, Carmel, New York 10512.

"Christmas in the Trenches" from the album *John McCutcheon: Live at Wolf Trap*. (Rounder Records) available from Appalseed Productions, 1025 Locust VA. Charlottesville, VA 22901. (c) 1990 by John McCutcheon/Appalsongs (ASCAP). Used by permission.

"POW Camp Brings Yule Meaning" by Harold Kinsch, published in the *Camarillo Daily News*. Copyright, *Ventura County Star*. Reprinted by permission.

V. `Twas the Night Before Christmas

"The Second Greatest Christmas Story Ever Told" by Thomas J. Burns. Reprinted with permission from the December 1989 *Reader's Digest*.

"Memories of Rudolph" by Barbara May Lewis as told to Carol Jearn Cook Coombs, February 2000.

Rudolph the Red-Nosed Reindeer by Robert L. May, (c) by Robert L. May. Published by Follett Publishing Company. Used by permission of Modern Curriculum Press.

VI. We Three Kings

"The Good King" by Natalie Babbitt. Published in *Redbook* magazine December 1971. Reprinted by permission of the author.

"The Other Wiseman" by Henry Van Dyke, adapted by Sterling W. Sill. (c) Church of Jesus Christ of Latter-day Saints. First published in *The Instructor*, December 1962. Used by permission.

"The Anniversary" by Margaret Sangster. Reprinted by permission of the Hearst Corporation.